The Inheritors

When William Golding was awarded the Nobel Prize in Literature, the Nobel Foundation said of his novels that they 'illuminate the human condition in the world of today'. Born in Cornwall in 1911, Golding was educated at Marlborough Grammar School and Brasenose College, Oxford. Before becoming a writer, he was an actor, a lecturer, a small-boat sailor, a musician and a schoolteacher. In 1940 he joined the Royal Navy and saw action against battleships, submarines and aircraft, and also took part in the pursuit of the *Bismarck*.

Lord of the Flies, his first novel, was rejected by several publishers and one literary agent. It was rescued from the 'slush pile' by a young editor at Faber and Faber and published in 1954. The book would go on to sell several million copies; it was translated into thirty-five languages and made into a film by Peter Brook in 1963. He wrote eleven other novels, *The Inheritors* and *The Spire* among them, a play and two essay collections. He won the Booker Prize for his novel *Rites of Passage* in 1980, and the Nobel Prize in Literature in 1983. He was knighted in 1988. He died at his home in the summer of 1993.

www.william-golding.co.uk

Books by
Sir William Golding
1911–1993
Nobel Prize in Literature

Fiction
LORD OF THE FLIES
THE INHERITORS
PINCHER MARTIN
FREE FALL
THE SPIRE
THE PYRAMID
THE SCORPION GOD
DARKNESS VISIBLE
THE PAPER MEN
RITES OF PASSAGE
CLOSE QUARTERS
FIRE DOWN BELOW
TO THE ENDS OF THE EARTH
(comprising *Rites of Passage*, *Close Quarters* and *Fire Down Below*
in a revised text; foreword by the author)
THE DOUBLE TONGUE

Essays
THE HOT GATES
A MOVING TARGET

Travel
AN EGYPTIAN JOURNAL

Plays
THE BRASS BUTTERFLY
LORD OF THE FLIES
adapted for the stage by Nigel Williams

WILLIAM GOLDING: A CRITICAL STUDY OF THE NOVELS
by Mark Kinkead-Weekes and Ian Gregor

WILLIAM GOLDING

The Inheritors

faber and faber

First published in 1955
by Faber and Faber Limited
Bloomsbury House
74–77 Great Russell Street
London WC1B 3DA
This paperback edition first published in 2011

Printed in England by CPI Bookmarque, Croydon

A CIP record for this book
is available from the British Library

The quotation from *Outline of History* by H. G. Wells is reprinted by
kind permission of his executors

ISBN 978–0–571–27358–4

Introduction

by John Carey

Golding always thought *The Inheritors* his best novel, and many critics agree. He wrote it very fast at a time when his career was taking off after years of rejection. In February 1954 Faber and Faber had at last agreed to publish *Lord of the Flies* (it came out on 17 September), and his editor, Charles Monteith, was eager to know what the next book would be. On 17 October Golding replied that he had written 'nearly a quarter' of a new novel. It was 'about H. Sapiens and H. Neanderthal', and he was getting on 'at a tremendous lick'.

Coming after a novel about schoolboys on a desert island, this new subject has been seen, and was seen by Monteith, as wildly erratic. But there are links between the two books. Both are about an encounter between civilization and savagery, and both suggest new ways of interpreting those terms. Both recount the killing of the innocent. The boys who turn savage in *Lord of the Flies* reflected Golding's interest in original sin and the fall, so it might seem natural for his next novel to enquire when the fall happened. Speaking to some Indian students many years later, he explained that his Neanderthals ('the people' in the novel) are unfallen because, unlike the 'new people' (*Homo sapiens*), they cannot think, they can only imagine: 'The Fall is thought'.

A note at the end of the manuscript records triumphantly, 'First draft finished 1315 on the 11th November in 29 days.' November the 11th was a Thursday in 1954, and the time – a quarter past one – reminds us that Golding wrote this and each of his first four novels during lunch hours, breaks and holidays while earning his living as a teacher at Bishop Wordsworth's School in Salisbury. The first draft is written in a green, hardcover Bishop Wordsworth's School exercise book using schoolmasterly red biro.

As often, Golding's wife Ann helped, or at least advised. Insertions in the manuscript read, 'Ann thinks Lok's fall too mysterious. People won't get it. I don't say clearly that Lok *smelt* what the old woman carried,' and, 'Ann says Fa should say "We are lucky by the sea. We can drink out of shells there."' This rather gives the lie to the letter Golding wrote on 31 November, explaining that he could not send Monteith the manuscript because his handwriting was illegible 'even to my wife'. Clearly he wanted time to rethink before submitting *The Inheritors* to Monteith's scrutiny. He promised to type it out over Christmas and send it then. 'I've learnt to compose at the typewriter, which is a help,' he added.

It was a help. He rewrote extensively as he typed, and the many differences between manuscript and typescript change the meaning of *The Inheritors*. At the end of the manuscript he had noted down things he needed to keep in mind for the rewrite. The first is that: 'The new people must be forced by *circumstances and their own natures* to destroy the people. Therefore the people must live on the only line of advance . . . They must come from somewhere (the sea?) and be going *to* somewhere.' In the rewrite the new people do come from the sea – Lok smells salt on their canoe – and they are going to the hunting grounds beyond the mountains.

The landscape in the rewrite would, Golding noted, have to be adjusted to fit this new idea: 'I begin to think of a great waterfall at the mouth of a gorge. Beyond the gorge a bit of river then a vast lake, surrounded by forest and plain.' The geography worried him, and he added a note: 'I must ask Jameson about a waterfall out of a gorge. Could the land beyond be a great crater? Against this, it would not be southern England.' John Jameson was the geography master at Bishop Wordsworth's, and Golding's consultation was evidently satisfactory. In the rewrite the waterfall does issue from a gorge, and upstream the river widens into a lake. Golding had based his description of the forest on memories of Savernake Forest near Marlborough, where his parents took him for walks as a child – hence his need to check that the geography was compatible with prehistoric southern England.

The waterfall, he notes at the end of the manuscript, is vital: 'The centre *symbol* is the waterfall, the time stream, the fall, the second law of thermodynamics. It must be vivid.' This ties in with what he told the Canadian critic Virginia Tiger – that he wrote the first draft as a rebuttal of the nineteenth-century doctrine of progress but, in the rewrite, stressed, on the contrary, the evolutionary life-force which drives the new people upwards 'at a higher level of energy' than the Neanderthals possess. This is symbolized by their ability to haul their canoes up past the waterfall and sail upriver against the current. Golding's reference to the second law of thermodynamics is clarified by a passage from his essay on Yeats.

The Satan of our cosmology is the Second Law of Thermodynamics which implies that everything is running down and will finally stop like an unwound clock. Life is in some sense a local contradiction of this law . . . we should be cheered when life refuses to submit to a general levelling down of energy and simply winds itself up again.

Water passing over the fall from a state of high to a state of low organization is an illustration of the second law. But the new people, defying the current, and pushed on by 'a new intensity, new vision', are a local contradiction of it. It is almost as if the first version of *The Inheritors* was written by the religious Golding, who mourns the destruction of innocent Neanderthals, and the revisions by his scientist father, who, as a keen believer in Darwinian evolution, might be expected to side with the intellectually superior new people.

Golding sent the typescript to Monteith on 15 February 1955, hedged with apologies. It was 'nowhere near final – hardly begun in fact'. Monteith should regard it as just 'a roughly shaped bit of marble or gritstone or putty', and if he could bear to 'skip through' it his criticisms would be of 'enormous value'. These disclaimers may seem overdone. But they reflect Golding's habitual nervousness about writing. In reply Monteith assured him that he was delighted with *The Inheritors*: it should be published as it stood.

His immediate reaction was anxiety, and he wrote by return to say he was 'a bit startled to find The Inheritors is finished'. What, he wondered, would an expert think of his depiction of Neanderthals? 'I haven't done any research for the book at all,' he warned, 'just brooded over what I know myself.' Should not some 'palaeontologist, anthropologist, archaeologist, hard-headed scientist' be consulted before publication? Monteith replied firmly that the book did not need an expert. 'If he had any suggestions to make they would be the wrong sort of suggestions.'

That was wise advice, given Golding's fragile self-confidence. But he was less ignorant than he made out. He had been fascinated by archaeology since childhood, had run the school archaeological society, and been on local digs. The landscape around Salisbury is rich in prehistory, and he recalls in an essay how he used to imagine coming face to face with a Neanderthal on his country walks. The speed with which he wrote the novel suggests a subject long pondered. What Neanderthals were really like was (and still is) disputed, but he was aware of the contending theories. He told Monteith that he had always found H. G. Wells's belief that they were gorilla-like monsters with cannibalistic tendencies 'uproariously funny', and he used Wells's statement derisively as the epigraph to his novel.

His own depiction of Neanderthal man and *Homo sapiens* reflects, to an extent, the archaeological evidence. His Neanderthals have no artefacts or containers, whereas the new people have necklaces, paintings, wine-skins and clay pots. Inventing containers (bags, baskets) was an important evolutionary step, since it allowed hunter-gatherers to bring back and store foodstuffs. Fa, the brightest Neanderthal, almost hits on the idea of containers when, watching the old woman cook broth in a deer's stomach and dip a stick in it to get it to Mal's mouth, she has an image of sea shells full of water. This was the incident Ann thought should be clarified, though Golding did not adopt her suggestion. Fa almost invents agriculture, too, when she imagines food growing on the terrace.

Neanderthals were hunter-gatherers, but Golding's are different. They gather the fruits of the forest but, because they have a sense that killing is 'wickedness', they depend for meat on what they can guiltily scavenge from kills made by big carnivores. Their language, which incorporates gesture, dance and a kind of telepathy, is another of Golding's innovations – among palaeontologists there is no general agreement that Neanderthals could speak. The new people practise shamanism, and their shaman, Marlan, is male, but Golding gives his Neanderthals a religion (the worship of a matriarchal goddess, Oa), and this was his widest divergence from received opinion. As he would have known, no traces of Neanderthal religion have been found; nor have any Neanderthal grave goods that would imply a belief in an afterlife. He gets round these possible objections by making his Neanderthals worship 'ice women', and place meat and water in the grave for the afterlife, none of which would leave any remnants for archaeologists to discover.

The admiration, almost love, that his Neanderthals feel for the new people may be his own idea, or he may have known there was archaeological evidence to support it. In Western Europe Neanderthals and *Homo sapiens* lived side by side for thousands of years, sometimes sharing the same sites, and there are indications that the Neanderthals imitated aspects of human culture, such as wearing ochre body paint, which has been taken to imply admiration.

The new people in the novel carry off a Neanderthal baby, giving hope that some vestige of the Neanderthals may survive in us. This was Golding's guess, but recent research supports it. In 2010 sequencing of the Neanderthal genome at Germany's Max Planck Institute revealed that up to 4 per cent of human DNA comes from Neanderthals, indicating a degree of cross-breeding between the two species.

The greatness of *The Inheritors* does not depend, however, on Golding imagining what Neanderthals might have been like. It depends on the language he fashions to express it. He accepts the colossal stylistic challenge of seeing everything from a Neanderthal point of view. By feats of language that are at first bewildering he takes us inside a being whose senses, especially smell and hearing, are acute, but who cannot connect sensations into a train of thought. This is a being whose awareness is a stream of metaphors and for whom everything is alive. Intricate verbal manoeuvres force us to share the adventures – and the pathos and the tragedy – of a consciousness that is fearless, harmless, loving, minutely observant and incapable of understanding anything. Though in prose, Golding's achievement is profoundly poetic, exemplifying T. S. Eliot's observation that the modern poet must become indirect 'in order to force, to dislocate if necessary, language into his meaning'.

The Inheritors was published on 16 September 1955, and reviewers instantly recognized its imaginative power and its originality. For Arthur Koestler it was 'an earthquake in the petrified forests of the English novel'. Half a century later, and however many times you have read it, it is still alarming, eye-opening, desolating, mind-invading and unique.

"... We know very little of the appearance of the Neanderthal man, but this ... seems to suggest an extreme hairiness, an ugliness, or a repulsive strangeness in his appearance over and above his low forehead, his beetle brows, his ape neck, and his inferior stature ... Says Sir Harry Johnston, in a survey of the rise of modern man in his *Views and Reviews:* 'The dim racial remembrance of such gorilla-like monsters, with cunning brains, shambling gait, hairy bodies, strong teeth, and possibly cannibalistic tendencies, may be the germ of the ogre in folklore ...' "

H. G. Wells, *Outline of History*

FOR ANN

ONE

Lok was running as fast as he could. His head was
down and he carried his thorn bush horizontally
for balance and smacked the drifts of vivid buds
aside with his free hand. Liku rode him laughing, one hand
clutched in the chestnut curls that lay on his neck and
down his spine, the other holding the little Oa tucked
under his chin. Lok's feet were clever. They saw. They
threw him round the displayed roots of the beeches, leapt
when a puddle of water lay across the trail. Liku beat
his belly with her feet.

"Faster! Faster!"

His feet stabbed, he swerved and slowed. Now they
could hear the river that lay parallel but hidden to their
left. The beeches opened, the bush went away and they
were in the little patch of flat mud where the log was.

"There, Liku."

The onyx marsh water was spread before them, widen-
ing into the river. The trail along by the river began again
on the other side on ground that rose until it was lost in
the trees. Lok, grinning happily, took two paces towards
the water and stopped. The grin faded and his mouth
opened till the lower lip hung down. Liku slid to his knee
then dropped to the ground. She put the little Oa's head
to her mouth and looked over her.

Lok laughed uncertainly.

I

"The log has gone away."

He shut his eyes and frowned at the picture of the log. It had lain in the water from this side to that, grey and rotting. When you trod the centre you could feel the water that washed beneath you, horrible water, as deep in places as a man's shoulder. The water was not awake like the river or the fall but asleep, spreading there to the river and waking up, stretching on the right into wildernesses of impassable swamp and thicket and bog. So sure was he of this log the people always used that he opened his eyes again, beginning to smile as if he were waking out of a dream; but the log was gone.

Fa came trotting along the trail. The new one was sleeping on her back. She did not fear that he would fall because she felt his hands gripping her hair at the neck and his feet holding the hair farther down her back but she trotted softly so that he should not wake. Lok heard her coming before she appeared under the beeches.

"Fa! The log has gone away!"

She came straight to the water's edge, looked, smelt, then turned accusingly to Lok. She did not need to speak. Lok began to jerk his head at her.

"No, no. I did not move the log to make the people laugh. It has gone."

He spread his arms wide to indicate the completeness of that absence, saw that she understood, and dropped them again.

Liku called him.

"Swing me."

She was reaching for a beech bough that came down out of the tree like a long neck, saw light and craned up with an armful of green and brown buds. Lok abandoned

2

the log that was not there and swung her into the crook. He heaved sideways, he pulled, gaining a little backwards with each step as the bough creaked.

"Ho!"

He let the branch go and dropped on to his hams. The bough shot away and Liku shrieked delightedly.

"No! No!"

But Lok hauled again and again and the armful of leaves bore Liku shrieking and laughing and protesting along the edge of the water. Fa was looking from the water to Lok and back. She was frowning again.

Ha came along the trail, hurrying but not running, more thoughtful than Lok, the man for an emergency. When Fa began to call out to him he did not answer her immediately but looked at the empty water and then away to the left where he could see the river beyond the arch of beeches. Then he searched the forest with ear and nose for intruders and only when he was sure of safety did he put down his thorn bush and kneel by the water.

"Look!"

His pointing finger showed the gashes under water where the log had moved. The edges were still sharp and pieces of broken earth lay in the gashes, not yet disintegrated by the water that covered them. He traced the curving gashes away down into the water until they disappeared in that obscurity. Fa looked across to the place where the broken trail began again. There was earth churned up there where the other end of the log had lain. She asked a question of Ha and he answered her with his mouth.

"One day. Perhaps two days. Not three."

Liku was still shrieking with laughter.

Nil came in sight along the trail. She was moaning gently as was her habit when tired and hungry. But though the skin was slack on her heavy body her breasts were stretched and full and the white milk stood in the nipples. Whoever else went hungry it would not be the new one. She glanced at him as he clung to Fa's hair, saw that he was asleep, then went to Ha and touched him on the arm.

"Why did you leave me? You have more pictures in your head than Lok."

Ha pointed to the water.

"I came quickly to see the log."

"But the log has gone away."

The three of them stood and looked at each other. Then, as so often happened with the people, there were feelings between them. Fa and Nil shared a picture of Ha thinking. He had thought that he must make sure the log was still in position because if the water had taken the log or if the log had crawled off on business of its own then the people would have to trek a day's journey round the swamp and that meant danger or even more discomfort than usual.

Lok flung all his weight against the bough and would not let it get away. He hushed Liku and she climbed down and stood by him. The old woman was coming along the trail, they could hear her feet and her breathing. She appeared round the last of the trunks, she was grey and tiny, she was bowed and remote in the contemplation of the leaf-wrapped burden that she carried in two hands by her withered breasts. The people stood together and their silence greeted her. She said nothing but waited with a sort of humble patience for what might come. Only the burden sagged a little in her hands and was lifted up again so that the people remembered how heavy it was.

Lok was the first to speak. He addressed them generally, laughing, hearing only words from his mouth but wanting laughter. Nil began to moan again.

Now they could hear the last of the people coming along the trail. It was Mal, coming slowly and coughing every now and then. He came round the last tree-trunk, stopped in the beginning of the open space, leaned heavily on the torn end of his thorn bush and began to cough. As he bent over they could see where the white hair had fallen away in a track that led from behind his eyebrows over his head and down into the mat of hair that lay across his shoulders. The people said nothing while he coughed but waited, still as deer at gaze, while the mud rose in square lumps that elongated and turned over between their toes. A sharply sculptured cloud moved away from the sun and the trees sifted chilly sunlight over their naked bodies.

At last Mal finished his cough. He began to straighten himself by bearing down on the thorn bush and by making his hands walk over each other up the stick. He looked at the water then at each of the people in turn, and they waited.

"I have a picture."

He freed a hand and put it flat on his head as if confining the images that flickered there.

"Mal is not old but clinging to his mother's back. There is more water not only here but along the trail where we came. A man is wise. He makes men take a tree that has fallen and——"

5

His eyes deep in their hollows turned to the people imploring them to share a picture with him. He coughed again, softly. The old woman carefully lifted her burden.

At last Ha spoke.

"I do not see this picture."

The old man sighed and took his hand away from his head.

"Find a tree that has fallen."

Obediently the people spread out along the water side. The old woman paced to the branch on which Liku had swung and rested her cupped hands on it. Ha was the first to call them. They hurried to him and winced at the liquid mud that rose to their ankles. Liku found some berries blackened and left over from the time of fruit. Mal came and stood, frowning at the log. It was the trunk of a birch, no thicker than a man's thigh, a trunk that was half-sunken in mud and water. The bark was peeling away here and there and Lok began to pull the coloured fungi from it. Some of the fungi were good to eat and Lok gave these to Liku. Ha and Nil and Fa plucked unhandily at the trunk. Mal sighed again

"Wait. Ha there. Fa there. Nil too. Lok!"

The log came up easily. There were branches left which caught in bushes, dragged in the mud and got in their way as they carried it heavily back to the dark neck of water. The sun hid again.

When they came to the edge of the water the old man stood frowning at the tumbled earth on the other side.

"Let the log swim."

This was delicate and difficult. However they handled the sodden wood their feet had to touch the water. At last the log lay floating and Ha was leaning out and holding the end. The other end sank a little. Ha began to bear with one hand and pull with the other. The branched head of the trunk moved out slowly and came to rest against the mud of the other side. Lok babbled happily in admiration, his head thrown back, words coming out at random. Nobody minded Lok, but the old man was frowning and pressing both hands on his head. The other end of the trunk was under water for perhaps twice the length of a man and that was the slimmest part. Ha looked his question at the old man who pressed his head again and coughed. Ha sighed and deliberately put a foot into the water. When the people saw what he was doing they groaned in sympathy. Ha inserted himself warily, he grimaced and the people grimaced with him. He gasped for breath, forcing himself in until the water washed over his knees and his hands gripped the rotten bark of the trunk till it rucked. Now he bore down with one hand and lifted with the other. The trunk rolled, the boughs stirred brown and yellow mud that swirled up with a shoal of turning leaves, the head lurched and was resting on a further bank. Ha pushed with all his strength but the splayed branches were too much for him. There was still a gap where the trunk curved under water on the farther side. He came back to the dry land, watched gravely by the people. Mal was looking at him expectantly, his two hands now holding the thorn bush again. Ha went to the place where the trail came into the open. He picked up his thorn bush and crouched. For a moment he leaned forward then as he fell his feet caught up with him and he was flashing across the open space. He took four paces on the log, falling all the time till it seemed his head must strike his knees; then the log

7

threshed up the water and Ha was flying through the air, feet drawn up and arms wide. He thumped on leaves and earth. He was over. He turned, seized the head of the trunk and hauled: and the trail was joined across the water.

The people cried out in relief and joy. The sun chose this moment to reappear so that the whole world seemed to share their pleasure. They applauded Ha, beating the flat of their hands against their thighs and Lok was sharing their triumph with Liku.

"Do you see, Liku? The trunk is across the water. Ha has many pictures!"

When they were quiet again Mal pointed his thorn bush at Fa.

"Fa and the new one."

Fa felt with her hand for the new one. The bunched hair by her neck covered him and they could see little but his hands and feet firmly gripped to individual curls. She went to the water's edge, stretched out her arms sideways and ran neatly across the trunk, jumped the last part and stood with Ha. The new one woke, peered out over her shoulder, shifted the grip of one foot and went to sleep again.

"Now Nil."

Nil frowned, drawing the skin together over her brows. She smoothed the curls back from them, she grimaced painfully and ran at the log. She held her hands high above her head and by the time she reached the middle she was crying out.

"Ai! Ai! Ai!"

The log began to bend and sink. Nil came to the thinnest part, leaped high, her full breasts bouncing and landed in water up to her knees. She screamed and lugged her feet out of the mud, seized Ha's outstretched hand and then was gasping and shuddering on the solid earth.

Mal walked to the old woman and spoke gently.

"Will she carry it across now?"

The old woman withdrew only in part from her inward contemplation. She paced down to the water's edge, still holding the two handfuls at breast height. There was little to her body but bone and skin and scanty white hair. When she walked swiftly across the trunk scarcely stirred in the water.

Mal bent down to Liku.

"Will you cross?"

Liku took the little Oa from her mouth and rubbed her mop of red curls against Lok's thigh.

"I will go with Lok."

This lit a kind of sunshine in Lok's head. He opened his mouth wide and laughed and talked at the people, though there was little connection between the quick pictures and the words that came out. He saw Fa laughing back at him and Ha smiling gravely.

Nil called out to them.

"Be careful, Liku. Hold tight."

Lok pulled a curl of Liku's hair.

"Up."

Liku took his hand, seized his knee with one foot and clambered to the curls of his back. The little Oa lay in her warm hand under his chin. She shouted at him.

"Now!"

Lok went right back to the trail under the beeches. He scowled at the water, rushed at it, then skidded to a stop. Across the water the people began to laugh. Lok rushed backwards and forwards, baulking each time at the near end of the log. He shouted.

"Look at Lok, the mighty jumper!"

Proudly he pranced forward, his pride diminished, he crouched and scuttled back. Liku was bouncing and shrieking.

"Jump! Jump!"

Her head was rolling helplessly against his. He came down to the water's edge as Nil, his hands high in the air.

"Ai! Ai!"

Even Mal was grinning at that. Liku's laughter had reached the silent, breathless stage and the water was falling from her eyes. Lok hid behind a beech tree and Nil held her breasts for laughter. Then suddenly Lok reappeared. He shot forward, head down. He flashed across the log with a tremendous shout. He leapt and landed on dry ground, bounced round and went on bouncing and jeering at the defeated water, till Liku began to hiccup by his neck and the people were holding on to each other.

At last they were silent and Mal came forward. He coughed a little and grimaced wryly at them.

"Now, Mal."

He held his thorn bush crossways for balance. He ran at the trunk, his old feet gripping and loosing. He began to cross, swaying the thorn bush about. He did not get up enough speed to cross in safety. They saw the anguish growing in his face, saw his bared teeth. Then his back foot pushed a piece of bark off the trunk and left a bare patch and he was not quick enough. The other foot slid and he fell forward. He bounced sideways and disappeared in a dirty flurry of water. Lok rushed up and down shouting as loud as he could.

"Mal is in the water!"

"Ai! Ai!"

Ha was wading in, grinning painfully at the strangeness of the cold touch. He got hold of the thorn bush, and Mal was on the other end. Now he had Mal by the wrist and they were falling about, seeming to wrestle with each other. Mal disengaged himself and began to crawl on all fours up the firmer ground. He got a beech tree between himself and the water and lay curled up and shuddering. The people gathered round in a tight little group. They crouched and rubbed their bodies against him, they wound their arms into a lattice of protection and comfort. The water streamed off him and left his hair in points. Liku wormed her way into the group and pressed her belly against his calves. Only the old woman still waited without moving. The group of people crouched round Mal and shared his shivers.

Liku spoke.

"I am hungry."

The people broke the knot round Mal and he stood up. He was still shivering. This shivering was not a surface movement of skin and hair but deep so that the very thorn bush shook with him.

"Come!"

He led the way along the trail. Here there was more space between the trees and many bushes in the spaces. They came presently to a clearing that a great tree had made before it died, a clearing close by the river and still dominated by the standing corpse of the tree. Ivy had taken over, its embedded stems making a varicose entanglement on the old trunk and ending where the trunk had branched in a huge nest of dark green leaves. Fungi had battened too, plates that stuck out and were full of rain-water, smaller jelly-like blobs of red and yellow so that the old tree was dissolving into dust and white pulp. Nil took food for Liku and Lok pried with his fingers for the white grubs. Mal waited for them. His body no longer shook all the time but jerked every now and then. After these jerks he would lean on his thorn bush as though he were sliding down it.

There was a new element present to the senses, a noise so steady and pervasive that the people did not need to remind each other what it was. Beyond the clearing the ground began to rise steeply, earthen, but dotted with smaller trees; and here the bones of the land showed, lumps of smooth grey rock. Beyond this slope was the gap through the mountains, and from the lip of this gap the river fell in a great waterfall twice the height of the tallest tree. Now they were silent the people attended to the distant drone of the water. They looked at each other and began to laugh and chatter. Lok explained to Liku.

"You will sleep to-night by the falling water. It has not gone away. Do you remember?"

"I have a picture of the water and the cave."

Lok patted the dead tree affectionately and Mal led them upward. Now in their joy they also began to pay attention to his weakness, though they were not yet aware how deep it was. Mal lifted his legs like a man pulling them out of mud and his feet were no longer clever. They chose places of their own unskilfully, but as though something were pulling them sideways so that he reeled on his stick. The people behind him followed each of his actions easily out of the fullness of their health. Focused on his struggle they became an affectionate and unconscious parody. As he leaned and reached for his breath they gaped too, they reeled, their feet were deliberately unclever. They wound up through a litter of grey boulders and knees of stone until the trees fell away and they were out in the open.

Here Mal stopped and coughed and they understood that now they must wait for him. Lok took Liku by the hand.

"See!"

The slope led up to the gap and the mountain rose before them. On the left the slope broke off and fell down a cliff to the river. There was an island in the river which extended up as though one part had been stood on end and leaned against the fall. The river fell over on both sides of the island, thinly on this side but most widely and tremendously on that; and where it fell no man could see for the spray and the drifting smoke. There were trees and thick bushes on the island but the end towards the fall was obscured as by a thick fog and the river on either side of it had only a qualified glitter.

Mal started off again. There were two ways up to the lip of the fall; one zigzagged away to their right and climbed among the rocks. Although that way would have been easier for Mal he ignored it as though he were anxious above all things to reach comfort quickly. He chose then the path to the left. Here were little bushes which held them up on the edge of the cliff, and while they were threading these Liku spoke to Lok again. The noise of the fall took the life out of her words and left nothing of them but a faint sketch.

"I am hungry."

Lok smacked himself on the chest. He shouted so that all the people heard.

"I have a picture of Lok finding a tree with ears that grow thickly——"

"Eat, Liku."

Ha stood by them with berries in his hand. He poured them out for Liku and she ate, burying her mouth in the food; and the little Oa lay uncomfortably under her arm. The food reminded Lok of his own hunger. Now they had left the dank winter cave by the sea and the bitter, unnatural tasting food of beach and salt marsh he had a sudden picture of good things, of honey and young shoots, of bulbs and grubs, of sweet and wicked meat. He picked up a stone and beat it on the barren rock by his head as presently he would beat on a likely tree.

Nil pulled a withered berry off the bush and put it in her mouth.

"See Lok beating a rock!"

When they laughed at him he clowned, pretending to listen to the rock and shouting.

"Wake up, grubs! Are you awake?"

But Mal was leading them onward.

The top of the cliff leaned back a little so that instead of climbing over the jagged top they could skirt the sheer part over the river where it ran out of the confusion at the foot of the falls. The trail gained height at each step, a dizzy way of slant and overhang, of gap and buttress where roughness to the foot was the only safety and the rock dived back under, leaving a void of air between them and the smoke and the island. Here the ravens floated below them like black scraps from a fire, the weed-tails wavered with only a faint glister over them to show where the water was: and the island, reared against the fall, interrupting the sill of dropping water, was separate as the moon. The cliff leaned out as if looking for its own feet in the water. The weed-tails were very long, longer than many men, and they moved backwards and forwards beneath the climbing people as regularly as the beat of a heart or the breaking of the sea.

Lok remembered how the ravens sounded. He flapped at them with his arms.

"Kwak!"

The new one stirred on Fa's back, shifting the grip of his hands and feet. Ha was going very slowly for his weight made him cautious. He crept along, hands and feet flexing and contracting on the slanting rock. Mal spoke again.

"Wait."

They read his lips as he turned to them and gathered in a group at his side. Here the trail expanded to a platform with room for them all. The old woman rested her hands on the slanting rock so that the weight was eased for her. Mal bent down and coughed till his shoulders were wrenched. Nil squatted by him, put one hand on his belly and the other on his shoulder.

Lok looked away over the river to forget his hunger. He flared his nostrils and immediately was rewarded with a whole mixture of smells, for the mist from the fall magnified any smell incredibly, as rain will deepen and distinguish the colours of a field of flowers. There were

15

the smells of the people too, individual but each engaged to the smell of the muddy path where they had been.

This was so concretely the evidence of their summer quarters that he laughed for joy and turned to Fa, feeling that he would like to lie with her for all his hunger. The rain-water from the forest had dried off her and the curls that clustered round her neck and over the new one's head were glossy red. He reached out his hand to her breast so that she laughed too and patted her hair back from her ears.

"We shall find food," he said with all of his wide mouth, "and we shall make love."

Mentioning food made his hunger as real as the smells. He turned again outwards to where he smelt the old woman's burden. Then there was nothing but emptiness and the smoke of the fall coming towards him from the island. He was down, spread-eagled on the rock, toes and hands gripping the roughness like limpets. He could see the weed-tails, not moving but frozen in an instant of extreme perception, beneath his armpit. Liku was squawking on the platform and Fa was flat by the edge, holding him by the wrist, while the new one struggled and whimpered in her hair. The other people were coming back. Ha was visible from the loins up, careful but swift and now leaning down to his other wrist. He felt the sweat of terror in their palms. A foot or a hand at a time he moved up until he was squatting on the platform. He scrambled round and gibbered at the weed-tails that were moving again. Liku was howling. Nil bent down and took her head between her breasts and stroked the curls down her back soothingly. Fa pulled Lok so that he faced her.

16

"Why?"

Lok knelt for a moment, scratching in the hair under his mouth. Then he pointed into the damp spray that was drifting at them across the island.

"The old woman. She was out there. And it."

The ravens were rising under his hand as the air poured up the cliff. Fa took her hand away from him when his man's voice touched the matter of the old woman. But Lok's eyes stayed on her face.

"She was out there——"

Complete incomprehension silenced them both. Fa was frowning again. She was not a woman to lie with. Something of the old woman was invisibly present in the air round her head. Lok implored her.

"I turned to her and fell."

Fa closed her eyes and spoke austerely.

"I do not see this picture."

Nil was leading Liku after the others. Fa followed them as if Lok did not exist. He clambered after her sheepishly aware of his mistake; but as he went he murmured:

"I turned to her——"

The others had gathered in a group farther along the path. Fa shouted to them.

"We are coming!"

Ha shouted back:

"There is an ice woman."

Beyond and above Mal there was a gully in the cliff loaded with old snow that the sun had not reached. Weight and cold and then the pelting rain of late winter had compacted the snow into ice that hung perilously and water ran out between the melting edge and the warmer rock. Though they had never seen an ice woman still left in this gully when they came back from their winter cave by the sea, the thought did not occur to them that Mal had taken them into the mountains too early. Lok forgot his escape and the strange indefinable newness of the spray-smell and ran forward. He stood by Ha and shouted:

"Oa! Oa! Oa!"

Ha and the others shouted with him.

"Oa! Oa! Oa!"

Over the insistent drumming of the fall their voices were puny and without resonance, yet the ravens heard and faltered, then glided smoothly once more. Liku was shouting and waving the little Oa, though she did not know why. The new one woke again, passed a pink tongue over his lips like a kitten and peered out from the curls by Fa's ear. The ice woman hung above and beyond them. Though the deadly water still trickled from her belly, she would not move. Then the people were silent and passed swiftly till she was hidden by the rock. They came without speech to the rocks by the fall where the huge cliff looked down for its feet in the turbulence and smother of white water. Almost on a level with their eyes was the clear curve where the water turned down over the sill, water so clear that they could see into it. There were weeds, not moving with slow rhythm but shivering madly as though anxious to be gone. Near the fall the rocks were wet with spray and ferns hung out over space. The people hardly glanced at the fall but pressed on quickly.

Above the fall the river came through a gap in the range of mountains.

Now that the day was almost done the sun lay in the gap and dazzled from the water. Across the water the current slid by sheer mountain that was black and hidden from the sun; but this side of the gap was less uncompromising. There was a slanting shelf, a terrace that gradually became a cliff. Lok ignored the unvisited island and the mountain beyond it on the other side of the gap. He began to hurry after the people as he remembered how safe the terrace was. Nothing could come at them out of the water because the current would snatch it over the fall; and the cliff above the terrace was for foxes, goats, the people, hyenas and birds. Even the way down from the terrace to the forest was defended by an entry so narrow that one man with a thorn bush could hold it. As for this trail on the sheer cliff above the spray pillars and the confusion of waters, it was worn by nothing but the feet of the people.

When Lok edged round the corner at the end of the trail the forest was already dark behind him, and shadows were racing through the gap towards the terrace. The people relaxed noisily on the terrace but then Ha swung his thorn bush so that the prickly head lay on the ground before him. He bent his knees and sniffed the air. At once the people were silent, spreading in a semicircle before the overhang. Mal and Ha stole forward, thorn bushes at the ready, moved up a little slope of earth until they could look down into the overhang.

But the hyenas had gone. Though the scent clung to the scattered stones that had dropped from the roof and the scanty grass that grew in the soil of generations, it was a day old. The people saw Ha lift his thorn bush until it was no longer a weapon and relaxed their muscles.

They moved a few paces up the slope and stood before the overhang while the sunlight threw their shadows sideways. Mal quelled the cough that rose from his chest, turned to the old woman and waited. She knelt in the overhang and laid the ball of clay in the centre of it. She opened the clay, smoothing and patting it over the old patch that lay there already. She put her face to the clay and breathed on it. In the very depth of the overhang there were recesses on either side of a pillar of rock and these were filled with sticks and twigs and thicker branches. She went quickly to the piles and came again with twigs and leaves and a log that was fallen almost to powder. She arranged this over the opened clay and breathed till a trickle of smoke appeared and a single spark shot into the air. The branch cracked and a flame of amethyst and red coiled up and straightened so that the side of her face away from the sun was glowing and her eyes gleamed. She came again from the recesses and put on more wood so that the fire gave them a brilliant display of flame and sparks. She began to work the wet clay with her fingers, tidying the edges so that now the fire sat in the middle of a shallow dish. Then she stood up and spoke to them.

"The fire is awake again."

TWO

At that the people talked again excitedly. They hurried into the hollow. Mal crouched down between the fire and the recess and spread out his hands, while Fa and Nil brought more wood and placed it ready. Liku brought a branch and gave it to the old woman. Ha squatted against the rock and shuffled his back till it fitted. His right hand found a stone and picked it up. He showed it to the people.

"I have a picture of this stone. Mal used it to cut a branch. See! Here is the part that cuts."

Mal took the stone from Ha, felt the weight, frowned a moment, then smiled at them.

"This is the stone I used," he said. "See! Here I put my thumb and here my hand fits round the thickness."

He held up the stone, miming Mal cutting a branch.

"The stone is a good stone," said Lok. "It has not gone away. It has stayed by the fire until Mal came back to it."

He stood up and peered over the earth and stones down the slope. The river had not gone away either or the mountains. The overhang had waited for them. Quite suddenly he was swept up by a tide of happiness and exultation. Everything had waited for them: Oa had waited for them. Even now she was pushing up the spikes of the bulbs, fattening the grubs, reeking the smells out of the earth, bulging the fat buds out of every crevice and bough. He danced on to the terrace by the river, his arms spread wide.

"Oa!"

Mal moved a little way from the fire and examined the back of the overhang. He peered at the surface and swept a few dried leaves and droppings from the earth at the base of the pillar. He squatted and shrugged his shoulders into place.

"And this is where Mal sits."

He touched the rock gently as Lok or Ha might touch Fa.

"We are home!"

Lok came in from the terrace. He looked at the old woman. Freed from the burden of the fire she seemed a little less remote, a little more like one of them. He could look her in the eye now and speak to her, perhaps even be answered. Besides, he felt the need to speak, to hide from the others the unease that the flames always called forth in him.

"Now the fire sits on the hearth. Do you feel warm Liku?"

Liku took the little Oa from her mouth.

"I am hungry."

"To-morrow we shall find food for all the people."

Liku held up the little Oa.

"She is hungry too."

"She shall go with you and eat."

He laughed round at the others.

"I have a picture——"

Then the people laughed too because this was Lok's picture, almost the only one he had, and they knew it as well as he did.

"—a picture of finding the little Oa."

Fantastically the old root was twisted and bulged and smoothed away by age into the likeness of a great-bellied woman.

"—I am standing among the trees. I feel. With this foot I feel——" He mimed for them. His weight was on his left foot and his right was searching in the ground. "—I feel. What do I feel? A bulb? A stick? A bone?" His right foot seized something and passed it to up his left hand. He looked. "It is the little Oa!" Triumphantly he sunned himself before them. "And now where Liku is there is the little Oa."

The people applauded him, grinning, half at Lok, half at the story. Secure in their applause, Lok settled himself by the fire and the people were silent, gazing into the flames.

The sun dropped into the river and light left the overhang. Now the fire was more than ever central, white ash, a spot of red and one flame wavering upwards The old woman moved softly, pushing in more wood so that the red spot ate and the flame grew strong. The people watched, their faces seeming to quiver in the unsteady light. Their freckled skins were ruddy and the deep caverns beneath their brows were each inhabited by replicas of the fire and all their fires danced together. As they persuaded themselves of the warmth they relaxed limbs and drew the reek into their nostrils gratefully. They flexed their toes and stretched their arms, even

23

leaning away from the fire. One of the deep silences fell on them, that seemed so much more natural than speech, a timeless silence in which there were at first many minds in the overhang; and then perhaps no mind at all. So fully discounted was the roar of the water that the soft touch of the wind on the rocks became audible. Their ears as if endowed with separate life sorted the tangle of tiny sounds and accepted them, the sound of breathing, the sound of wet clay flaking and ashes falling in.

Then Mal spoke with unusual diffidence.

"It is cold?"

Called back into their individual skulls they turned to him. He was no longer wet and his hair curled. He moved forward decisively and knelt so that his knees were on the clay, his arms as supports on either side and the full heat beating on his chest. Then the spring wind flicked at the fire and sent the thin column of smoke straight into his open mouth. He choked and coughed. He went on and on, the coughs seeming to come out of his chest without warning or consultation. They threw his body about and all the time he gaped for his breath. He fell over sideways and his body began to shake. They could see his tongue and the fright in his eyes.

The old woman spoke.

"This is the cold of the water where the log was."

She came and knelt by him and rubbed his chest with her hands and kneaded the muscles of his neck. She took his head on her knees and shielded him from the wind till his coughing was done and he lay still, shivering slightly. The new one woke up and scrambled down from Fa's back. He crawled among the stretched legs with his red thatch glistening in the light. He saw the fire, slipped under Lok's raised knee, took hold of Mal's ankle and pulled himself upright. Two little fires lit in his eyes and he stayed, leaning forward, holding on to the shaking leg. The people divided their attention between him and Mal. Then a branch burst so that Lok jumped and sparks shot out into the darkness. The new one was on all fours before the sparks landed. He scuttled among the legs, climbed Nil's arm and hid himself in the hair of her back and neck. Then one of the little fires appeared by her left ear, an unwinking fire that watched warily. Nil moved her face sideways and rubbed her cheek gently up and down on the baby's head. The new one was enclosed again. His own thatch and his mother's curls made a cave for him. Her mop hung down and sheltered him. Presently the tiny point of fire by her ear went out.

Mal pulled himself up so that he sat leaning against the old woman. He looked at each of them in turn. Liku opened her mouth to speak but Fa hushed her quickly.

Now Mal spoke.

"There was the great Oa. She brought forth the earth from her belly. She gave suck. The earth brought forth woman and the woman brought forth the first man out of her belly."

They listened to him in silence. They waited for more, for all that Mal knew. There was the picture of the time when there had been many people, the story that they all liked so much of the time when it was summer all year round and the flowers and fruit hung on the same branch. There was also a long list of names that began at Mal and went back choosing always the oldest man of the people at that time: but now he said nothing more.

Lok sat between him and the wind.

"You are hungry, Mal. A man who is hungry is a cold man."

Ha lifted up his mouth.

"When the sun comes back we will get food. Stay by the fire, Mal, and we will bring you food and you will be strong and warm."

Then Fa came and leaned her body against Mal so that three of them shut him in against the fire. He spoke to them between coughs.

"I have a picture of what is to be done."

He bowed his head and looked into the ashes. The people waited. They could see how his life had stripped him. The long hairs on the brow were scanty and the curls that should have swept down over the slope of his skull had receded till there was a finger's-breadth of naked and wrinkled skin above his brows. Under them the great eye-hollows were deep and dark and the eyes in them dull and full of pain. Now he held up a hand and inspected the fingers closely.

"People must find food. People must find wood."

He held his left fingers with the other hand; he gripped them tightly as though the pressure would keep the ideas inside and under control.

"A finger for wood. A finger for food."

He jerked his head and started again.

"A finger for Ha. For Fa. For Nil. For Liku——"

He came to the end of his fingers and looked at the other hand, coughing softly. Ha stirred where he sat but said nothing. Then Mal relaxed his brow and gave up. He bowed down his head and clasped his hands in the grey hair at the back of his neck. They heard in his voice how tired he was.

"Ha shall get wood from the forest. Nil will go with him, and the new one." Ha stirred again and Fa moved her arm from the old man's shoulders, but Mal went on speaking.

"Lok will get food with Fa and Liku."

Ha spoke:

"Liku is too little to go on the mountain and out on the plain!"

Liku cried out:

"I will go with Lok!"

Mal muttered under his knees:

"I have spoken."

Now the thing was settled the people became restless. They knew in their bodies that something was wrong, yet the word had been said. When the word had been said it was as though the action was already alive in performance and they worried. Ha clicked a stone aimlessly against the rock of the overhang and Nil was moaning softly again. Only Lok, who had fewest pictures, remembered the blinding pictures of Oa and her bounty that had set him dancing on the terrace. He jumped up and faced the people and the night air shook his curls.

"I shall bring back food in my arms"—he gestured hugely—"so much food that I stagger—so!"

Fa grinned at him.

"There is not as much food as that in the world."

He squatted.

"Now I have a picture in my head. Lok is coming back to the fall. He runs along the side of the mountain. He carries a deer. A cat has killed the deer and sucked its blood, so there is no blame. So. Under this left arm.

And under this right one"—he held it out—"the quarters of a cow."

He staggered up and down in front of the overhang under the load of meat. The people laughed with him, then at him. Only Ha sat silent, smiling a little until the people noticed him and looked from him to Lok.

Lok blustered:

"That is a true picture!"

Ha said nothing with his mouth but continued to smile. Then as they watched him, he moved both ears round, slowly and solemnly aiming them at Lok so that they said as clearly as if he had spoken: I hear you! Lok opened his mouth and his hair rose. He began to gibber wordlessly at the cynical ears and the half-smile.

Fa interrupted them.

"Let be. Ha has many pictures and few words. Lok has a mouthful of words and no pictures."

At that Ha shouted with laughter and wagged his feet at Lok and Liku laughed without knowing why. Lok yearned suddenly for the mindless peace of their accord. He put his fit of temper on one side and crept back to the fire, pretending to be very miserable so that they pretended to comfort him. Then there was silence again and one mind or no mind in the overhang.

Quite without warning, all the people shared a picture inside their heads. This was a picture of Mal, seeming a little removed from them, illuminated, sharply defined in all his gaunt misery. They saw not only Mal's body but the slow pictures that were waxing and waning in his head. One above all was displacing the others, dawning through the cloudy arguments and doubts and conjectures until they knew what it was he was thinking with such dull conviction.

"To-morrow or the day after, I shall die."

The people became separate again. Lok stretched out his hand and touched Mal. But Mal did not feel the touch in his pain and under the woman's sheltering hair. The old woman glanced at Fa.

"It is the cold of the water."

She bent and whispered in Mal's ear:

"To-morrow there will be food. Now sleep."

Ha stood up.

"There will be more wood too. Will you not give the fire more to eat?"

The old woman went to a recess and chose wood. She fitted these pieces cunningly together till wherever the flames rose they found dry wood to bite on. Soon the flames were beating at the air and the people moved back into the overhang. This enlarged the semicircle and Liku slipped into it. Hair crinkled in warning and the people smiled at each other in delight. Then they began to yawn widely. They arranged themselves round Mal, huddling in, holding him in a cradle of warm flesh with the fire in front of him. They shuffled and muttered. Mal coughed a little, then he too was asleep.

Lok squatted to one side and looked out over the dark waters. There had been no conscious decision but he was on watch. He yawned too and examined the pain in his belly. He thought of good food and dribbled a little and was about to speak but then he remembered that they were all asleep. He stood up instead and scratched the close curls under his lip. Fa was within reach and suddenly he desired her again; but this desire was easy to forget because most of his mind preferred to think about food instead. He remembered the hyenas and padded along the terrace until he could look down the slope to the forest. Miles of darkness and sooty blots stretched away to the grey bar that was the sea; nearer, the river shone dispersedly in swamps and meanders. He looked up at the sky and saw that it was clear except where layers of fleecy cloud lay above the sea. As he watched and the after-image of the fire faded he saw a star prick open. Then there were others, a scatter, fields of quivering lights from horizon to horizon. His eyes considered the stars without blinking, while his nose searched for the hyenas and told him that they were nowhere near. He clambered over the rocks and looked down at the fall. There was always light where the river fell into its basin. The smoky spray seemed to trap whatever light there was and to dispense it subtly. Yet this light illumined nothing but the spray so that the island was total darkness. Lok gazed without thought at the black trees and rocks that loomed through the dull whiteness. The island was like the whole leg of a seated giant, whose knee, tufted with trees and bushes, interrupted the glimmering sill of the waterfall and whose ungainly foot was splayed out down there, spread, lost likeness and joined the dark wilderness. The giant's thigh that should have supported a body like a mountain, lay in the sliding water of the gap and diminished till it ended in disjointed rocks that curved to within a few men's lengths of the terrace. Lok considered the giant's thigh as he might have considered the moon: something so remote that it had no connection with life as he knew it. To reach the island the people would have to leap that gap between the terrace and the rocks across water that was eager to snatch them over the fall. Only some creature more agile and frightened would dare that leap. So the island remained unvisited.

A picture came to him in his relaxation of the cave by the sea and he turned to look down river. He saw the meanders as pools that glistened dully in the darkness. Odd pictures came to him of the trail that led all the way from the sea to the terrace through the gloom below him. He looked and grew confused at the thought that the trail was really there where he was looking. This part of the country with its confusion of rocks that seemed to be arrested at the most tempestuous moment of swirling, and that river down there spilt among the forest were too complicated for his head to grasp, though his senses could find a devious path across them. He abandoned thought with relief. Instead he flared his nostrils, and searched for the hyenas but they were gone. He pattered down to the edge of the rock and made water into the river. Then he went back softly and squatted to one side of the fire. He yawned once, desired Fa again, scratched himself. There were eyes watching him from the cliffs, eyes even, on the island, but nothing would come nearer while the ashes of the fire still glowed. As though she were conscious of his thought the old woman woke, put on a little wood and began to rake the ashes together with a flat stone. Mal coughed dryly in his sleep so that the others stirred. The old woman settled again and Lok put his palms into the hollows of his eyes and rubbed them sleepily. Green spots from the pressure floated across the river. He blinked to the left where the waterfall thundered so monotonously that already he could no longer hear it. The wind moved on the water, hovered; and then came strongly up from the forest and through the gap. The sharp line of the horizon blurred and the forest lightened. There was a cloud rising over the waterfall, mist stealing up from the sculptured basin, the pounded river water being thrown back by the wind. The island dimmed, the wet mist stole towards the terrace, hung under the arch of the overhang and enveloped the people in drops that were too small to be felt and could only be seen in numbers. Lok's nose opened automatically and sampled the complex of odours that came with the mist.

He squatted, puzzled and quivering. He cupped his hands over his nostrils and examined the trapped air. Eyes shut, straining attention, he concentrated on the touch of the warming air, seemed for a moment on the very brink of revelation; then the scent dried away like water, dislimned like a far-off small thing when the tears of effort drown it. He let the air go and opened his eyes. The mist of the fall was drifting away with a change of wind and the smell of the night was ordinary.

He frowned at the island and the dark water that slid towards the lip, then yawned. He could not hold a new thought when there seemed no danger in it. The fire was sinking to a red eye that lit nothing but itself and the people were still and rock-coloured. He settled down and leaned forward to sleep, pressing his nostrils in with one hand so that the stream of cold air was diminished. He drew his knees to his chest and presented the least possible surface to the night air. His left arm stole up and insinuated the fingers in the hair at the back of his neck. His mouth sank on his knees.

Over the sea in a bed of cloud there was a dull orange

light that expanded. The arms of the clouds turned to gold and the rim of the moon nearly at the full pushed up among them. The sill of the fall glittered, lights ran to and fro along the edge or leapt in a sudden sparkle. The trees on the island acquired definition, the birch trunk that overtopped them was suddenly silver and white. Across the water on the other side of the gap the cliff still harboured the darkness but everywhere else the mountains exhibited their high snow and ice. Lok slept, balanced on his hams. A hint of danger would have sent him flying along the terrace like a sprinter from his mark. Frost twinkled on him like the twinkling ice of the mountain. The fire was a blunted cone containing a handful of red over which blue flames wandered and plucked at the unburnt ends of branches and logs.

The moon rose slowly and almost vertically into a sky where there was nothing but a few spilled traces of cloud. The light crawled down the island and made the pillars of spray full of brightness. It was watched by green eyes, it discovered grey forms that slid and twisted from light to shadow or ran swiftly across the open spaces on the sides of the mountain. It fell on the trees of the forest so that a scatter of faint ivory patches moved over the rotting leaves and earth. It lay on the river and the wavering weed-tails; and the water was full of tinsel loops and circles and eddies of liquid cold fire. There came a noise from the foot of the fall, a noise that the thunder robbed of echo and resonance, the form of a noise. Lok's ears twitched in the moonlight so that the frost that lay along their upper edges shivered. Lok's ears spoke to Lok.

"?"

But Lok was asleep.

THREE

Lok was aware of the old woman moving earlier than any of them, busy about the fire in the first dawn light. She built up a pile of wood and in his sleep he heard the wood begin to burst and crackle. Fa was still crouched and the old man's head stirred on her shoulder restlessly. Ha moved and stood up. He went down the terrace and made water, then came back and looked at the old man. Mal was not waking like the others. He sat heavily on his hams, turning his head from side to side in Fa's hair and breathing quickly as a doe when she is heavy with young. His mouth was open wide to the hot fire; but another fire that was invisible was melting him away; it lay everywhere on the sunken flesh of his limbs and round the hollows of his eyes. Nil ran down to the river and brought water in her cupped hands. Mal sucked the water in before his eyes were open. The old woman put more wood on the fire. She pointed into the recess and jerked her head at the forest. Ha touched Nil on the shoulder.

"Come!"

The new one woke too, scrambled over Nil's shoulder, mewed at her a moment, then was at her breast. Nil padded after Ha towards the quick way down to the forest while the new one milked her. They edged round the corner and disappeared into the morning mist that lay almost level with the top of the fall.

34

Mal opened his eyes. They had to lean down to him before they could hear what he said.

"I have a picture."

The three people waited. Mal raised a hand and put it flat on top of his head above the eyebrows. Though two fires were shaking in his eyes he was not looking at them but at something far away across the water. So intent and fearful was this attention that Lok turned to see if he could find what Mal was frightened of. There was nothing: only a log, moved from some creeky shore of the river by the spring flood slid past them and up-ended noiselessly over the lip of the fall.

"I have a picture. The fire is flying away into the forest and eating up the trees."

His breathing was quicker now he was awake.

"It is burning. The forest is burning. The mountain is burning——"

His head turned to each of them. There was panic in his voice.

"Where is Lok?"

"Here."

Mal screwed up his eyes at him, frowning and bewildered.

"Who is this? Lok is on his mother's back and the trees are eaten."

Lok shifted his feet and laughed foolishly. The old woman took Mal's hand and raised it to her cheek.

"That is a picture of long ago. That is all done. You have seen it in your sleep."

Fa patted his shoulder. Then her hand stayed against the skin and her eyes opened wide. But she spoke to Mal gently as she might have spoken to Liku.

"Lok is standing on his feet before you. See! He is a man."

Relieved to understand at last, Lok spoke quickly to all of them.

"Yes, I am a man." He spread out his hands. "Here I am, Mal."

Liku woke, yawning, and the little Oa fell off her shoulder. She put it to her chest.

"I am hungry."

Mal turned so quickly that he nearly fell away from Fa and she had to grab him.

"Where are Ha and Nil?"

"You sent them," said Fa. "You sent them for wood. And Lok and Liku and me for food. We will bring some for you quickly."

Mal rocked to and fro, his face in his hands.

"That is a bad picture."

The old woman put her arms round him.

"Now sleep."

Fa drew Lok away from the fire.

"It is not good that Liku should come out on the plain with us. Let her stay by the fire."

"Mal said."

"He is sick in his head."

"He saw all things burning. I was afraid. How can the mountain burn?"

Fa spoke defiantly.

"To-day is like yesterday and to-morrow."

Ha and Nil with the new one laboured through the entry to the terrace. They bore armfuls of broken branches. Fa ran to them.

"Must Liku come with us because Mal said so?"

36

Ha pulled at his lip.

"That is a new thing. But it was spoken."

"Mal saw the mountain burning."

Ha looked up at the great dim height above them.

"I do not see this picture."

Lok giggled nervously.

"To-day is like yesterday and to-morrow."

Ha twitched his ears at them and smiled gravely.

"It was spoken."

All at once the indefinable tension broke and Fa, Lok and Liku ran swiftly along the terrace. They leapt at the cliff and began to clamber up. Directly they were high enough to see the line of smoky spray at the foot of the fall the noise of it hit them. When the cliff leaned back a little, Lok went down on one knee, and shouted.

"Up!"

The light was brighter now. They could see the shining river where it lay in the gap through the mountains and the vast stretches of fallen sky where the mountains dammed back the lake. Below them the mist hid the forest and the plain and rested quietly against the side of the mountain. They began to run along the steep side, flitting down towards the mist. They passed across the bare rock and reached high screes of broken and sharp stones, clambered down crazy gullies until they came to rounded rocks where there was a scant fledging of grass and a few bushes that leaned away from the wind. The grass was wet and spiders' webs hitched across the blades broke and clung to their ankles. The slope decreased, the bushes were more frequent. They were coming down to the limit of the mist.

"The sun will drink up the mist."

Fa paid no attention. She was questing, head down, so that the curls by her cheek brushed drops of water from the leaves. A bird squawked and blundered heavily away into the air. Fa pounced on the nest and Liku beat her feet against Lok's belly.

"Eggs! Eggs!"

She slipped from his back and danced among the tufts of grass. Fa broke a thorn from a bush and pierced the egg at both ends. Liku snatched it from her hands and began to suck noisily. There was an egg for Fa and one for Lok. All three were empty between two breathings. When they had eaten them the people knew how hungry they were and began to search busily. They went forward, bent and questing. Though they did not look up they knew that they were following the retreating mist down on to the level ground and that towards the sea the luminous opacity contained the first rays of the sun. They parted leaves and peered into bushes, they found the un-awakened grubs, the pale shoots that lay under a load of stone. As they worked and ate Fa consoled them.

"Ha and Nil will bring a little food from the forest."

Lok was finding grubs, soft delicacies full of strength.

"We cannot go back with a single grub. And back. And then a single grub."

Then they came into an open space. A stone had fallen from the mountain and struck another from its place. The patch of bare earth had been invaded by fat white shoots that had broken into the light, yet were so short and thick that they snapped at a touch. Side by side they concentrated on the circle, eating in. There was so much that they talked as they ate, brief ejaculations of pleasure and excitement, there was so much that for a while they ceased to feel famished and were only hungry. Liku said nothing but sat with her legs stretched out and ate with both hands.

Presently Lok made an embracing gesture.

"If we eat at this end of the patch then we can bring the people to eat at that end."

Fa spoke indistinctly.

"Mal will not come and she will not leave him. We shall come back this way when the sun goes the other side of the mountain. We will take to the people what we can carry in our arms."

Lok belched at the patch and looked at it affectionately.

"This is a good place."

Fa frowned and munched.

"If the patch were nearer——"

She swallowed her mouthful with a gulp.

"I have a picture. The good food is growing. Not here. It is growing by the fall."

Lok laughed at her.

"No plant like this grows near the fall!"

Fa put her hands wide apart, watching Lok all the time. Then she began to bring them together. But though the tilt of her head, the eyebrows moved slightly up and apart asked a question she had no words with which to define it. She tried again.

"But if—— See this picture. The overhang and the fire is down here."

Lok lifted his face away from his mouth and laughed.

"This place is down here. And the overhang and the fire is there."

He broke off more shoots, stuffed them into his mouth

39

and went on eating. He looked into the clearer sunlight and read the signs of the day. Presently Fa forgot her picture and stood up. Lok stood up too and spoke for her.

"Come!"

They padded down among the rocks and bushes. All at once the sun was through, a round of dulled silver, racing slantwise through the clouds yet always staying in the same place. Lok went first, then Liku, serious and eager on this her first proper food hunt. The slope eased and they reached the cliff-like border that gave on to the heathery sea of the plain. Lok poised and the others stilled behind him. He turned, looked a question at Fa, then raised his head again. He blew out air through his nose suddenly, then breathed in. Delicately he sampled this air, drawing a stream into his nostrils and allowing it to remain there till his blood had warmed it and the scent was accessible. He performed miracles of perception in the cavern of his nose. The scent was the smallest possible trace. Lok, if he had been capable of such comparisons, might have wondered whether the trace was a real scent or only the memory of one. So faint and stale was this scent that when he looked his question at Fa she did not understand him. He breathed the word at her.

"Honey?"

Liku jumped up and down till Fa hushed her. Lok tried the air again but this time a new coil of it came to him and this was empty. Fa waited.

Lok did not need to think where the wind was coming from. He clambered on to an apron of rock that held its area out to the sun and began to cast across it. The direction of the wind changed and the scent touched him again. The scent became excitingly real and soon he was following it to a little cliff that frost and sun had fissured and rain worn into a mesh of crevices. There were stains round one of these like the marks of brown fingers, and a single bee, hardly alive, though the sun shone full on the rock-face, was clinging perhaps a hand's-breadth from the opening. Fa jerked her head.

"There will be little honey."

Lok reversed his thorn bush and pushed the torn butt into the crack. A few bees began to hum dully, drugged by cold and hunger. Lok levered the butt about in the crack. Liku was hopping.

"Is there honey, Lok? I want honey!"

Bees crawled out of the crack and lumbered round them. Some fell heavily to the ground and crawled with fanning wings. One hung in Fa's hair. Lok drew the stick back. There was a little honey and wax on the end. Liku stopped jumping and began to lick the butt clean. Now that the others had dulled the point of their hunger they could enjoy watching Liku eat.

Lok chattered.

"Honey is best. There is strength in honey. See how Liku likes honey. I have a picture of the time when honey will run out of this crack in the rock so that you can taste honey off your fingers—so!"

He smeared his hand down the rock, licked his fingers and tasted the memory of honey. Then he thrust the butt into the crack again so that Liku might eat. Presently Fa became restless.

"This is old honey from the time when we went down to the sea. We must find more food for the others. Come!"

But Lok was thrusting the butt in again for joy of

Liku's eating, the sight of her belly and the memory of honey. Fa went away down the apron of rock, following the mist as it sucked back to the plain. She lowered herself over the edge and was out of sight. Then they heard her cry out. Liku scrambled up on Lok's back and he flitted down the apron towards the cry with his thorn bush at the ready. At the edge of the apron was a jagged gully that led out to the open country. Fa was crouching in the mouth of this gully, looking out over the grass and heather of the plain. Lok raced to her. Fa was trembling slightly and raised on her toes. There were two yellowish creatures out there, their legs hidden by the brown bushes of heather, near enough for her to see their eyes. They were prick-eared animals, roused by her voice from their business and standing now at gaze. Lok slid Liku from his back.

"Climb."

Liku scrambled up the side of the gully and squatted, higher in the air than Lok could reach. The yellow creatures showed their teeth.

"Now!"

Lok stole forward holding his thorn bush sideways. Fa circled out to his left. She carried a natural blade of stone in either hand. The two hyenas moved closer together and snarled. Fa suddenly jerked her right hand round and the stone thumped the bitch in the ribs. The bitch yelped then ran howling. Lok shot forward, swinging the thorn bush, and thrust the spines at the dog's snarling muzzle. Then the two beasts were out of reach, talking evilly and afraid. Lok stood between them and the kill.

"Be quick, I smell cat."

42

Fa was already down on her knees, struggling with the limp body.

"A cat has sucked all her blood. There is no blame. The yellow ones have not even reached the liver."

She was tearing fiercely at the doe's belly with the flake of stone. Lok brandished his thorn bush at the hyenas.

"There is much food for all the people."

He could hear how Fa grunted and gasped as she tore at the furred skin and the guts.

"Be quick."

"I cannot."

The hyenas, having finished their evil talk, were circling forward to left and right. Shadows flitted across Lok as he faced them from two great birds that were floating in the air.

"Take the doe to the rock."

Fa began to lug at the doe, then cried out in anger at the hyenas. Lok backed to her, bent down, seized the doe by the leg. He began to drag the body heavily towards the gully, brandishing the thorn bush the while. Fa seized a foreleg and hauled too. The hyenas followed them, keeping always just out of reach. The people got the doe into the narrow entrance to the gully just below Liku and the two birds floated down. Fa began to slash again with her splinter of stone. Lok found a boulder which he could use hammer-wise. He began to pound at the body, breaking out the joints. Fa was grunting with excitement. Lok talked as his great hands tore and twisted and snapped the sinews. All the time the hyenas ran to and fro. The birds drifted in and settled on the rock opposite Liku so that she slithered down to Lok and Fa.

43

The doe was wrecked and scattered. Fa split open her belly, slit the complicated stomach and spilt the sour cropped grass and broken shoots on the earth. Lok beat in the skull to get at the brain and levered open the mouth to wrench away the tongue. They filled the stomach with tit-bits and twisted up the guts so that the stomach became a floppy bag.

All the while, Lok talked between his grunts.

"This is bad. This is very bad."

Now the limbs were smashed and bloodily jointed Liku crouched by the doe eating the piece of liver that Fa had given her. The air between the rocks was forbidding with violence and sweat, with the rich smell of meat and wickedness.

"Quick! Quick!"

Fa could not have told him what she feared; the cat would not come back to a drained kill. It would be already half a day's journey away over the plain, hanging round the skirts of the herd, perhaps racing forward to sink its sabres in the neck of another victim and suck the blood. Yet there was a kind of darkness in the air under the watching birds.

Lok spoke loudly, acknowledging the darkness.

"This is very bad. Oa brought the doe out of her belly."

Fa muttered through her clenched teeth as her hands tore.

"Do not speak of that one."

Liku was still eating, unmindful of the darkness, eating the rich warm liver till her jaws ached. After Fa's rebuke, Lok no longer chattered but muttered instead.

"This is bad. But a cat killed you so there is no blame."

And as he moved his wide lips he dribbled.

The sun had cleared the mist now and they could see beyond the hyenas the heathery undulations of the plain and beyond it the lower level of light green tree-tops and the flash of water. Behind them the mountains sloped up, austere. Fa squatted back and got her breath. She rubbed the back of one hand across her brows.

"We must go high where the yellow ones cannot follow."

There was little left of the doe but torn hide, bones and hoofs. Lok handed his thorn bush to Fa. She swished it in the air and shouted rude things at the hyenas. Lok laced the haunches together with twisted gut then wound the end round his wrist so that he could hold them with one hand. He bent down and took the tail of the stomach in his teeth. Fa had an armful and he a double embrace of torn and quivering fragments. He began to retreat, grunting and fierce. The hyenas moved into the mouth of the gully, the buzzards flapped up and circled just out of reach of the bush. Liku, very bold between the man and woman, flopped her piece of liver at the buzzards.

"Go away, beaks! This is Liku's meat!"

The buzzards screamed, gave up, and went to argue with the hyenas who were crunching the split bones and the bloody hide. Lok could not talk. The food from the doe was as much as he could have carried on level ground as a proper load over the shoulder. Now it hung from him, bearing mostly against the grip of his fingers and his clenched teeth. Before they reached the top of the apron he was bending and there was pain in his wrists. But Fa understood this without sharing a picture. She came to him and took away the floppy stomach so that

45

he could gasp easily. Then she and Liku climbed on ahead, leaving him to follow. He arranged the meat in three different ways before he could labour after them. There was such a mixture of darkness and joy in his head that he heard his heart beating. He talked to the darkness that had lain over the mouth of the gully.

"There is little food when the people come back from the sea. There are not yet berries nor fruit nor honey nor almost anything to eat. The people are thin with hunger and they must eat. They do not like the taste of meat but they must eat."

Now he was padding along the side of the mountain on a slope of smooth rock where he depended on the grip of his feet. Still dribbling as he swayed along the high rocks he added a brilliant thought.

"The meat is for Mal who is sick."

Fa and Liku found a fault in the mountain side and began to trot onward to the gap. Lok was left far behind, labouring along and looking for a rock on which he might rest his meat as the old woman had rested the fire. He found one where the fault began, a table spread and emptiness on the other side. He squatted and let the meat slither till it bore its own weight. Below and behind, the buzzards had been joined by others and an angry party was in progress. He turned away from the gully and its darkness and looked for Fa and Liku. They were far ahead, still trotting towards the gap where they would tell the others of the food and perhaps send Ha back to help him carry it. He was disinclined to go forward again and rested for a while watching the busy world. The sky was light blue and the distant bar of the sea not much darker. The darkest things to be seen were patches of

46

deep blue shadow moving towards him over the grass and stone and heather, over the grey outcroppings of the plain. Where they rested on the trees of the forest they damped down the green mists of spring foliage and took the flash out of the river. As they came nearer the mountain they widened in extent and dragged over the crest. He looked along towards the fall where Fa and Liku were tiny figures about to duck out of sight. Then he began to frown at the air over the fall and his mouth opened. The smoke of the fire had moved and changed in quality. For a moment he thought that the old woman had shifted it but then the folly of this picture made him laugh. Neither would the old woman make smoke like that. It was a coil of yellow and white, the smoke that comes from wet wood or a green branch loaded with leaves; no one but a fool or some creature too unacquainted with the nature of fire would use it so unwisely. The idea of two fires came to him. Fire sometimes fell from the sky and flared in the forest for a while. It woke magically on the plain among the heather when the flowers had died away and the sun was too hot.

Lok laughed again at his picture. The old woman would not make such smoke and fires never woke of their own accord in the wet spring. He watched the smoke uncoil and drift away through the gap, thinning as it went. Then he smelt meat and forgot the smoke and his picture. He gathered up the lumps and staggered after Fa and Liku along the fault. The weight of the meat, and the thought of bringing all this food back to the people and their respect for the bringer kept the pictures of the smoke out of his head. Fa came running back along the fault. She took some of the lumps from his arms and they half-climbed, half-slithered down the last slope.

Smoke was rolling heavily from the overhang, blue, hot smoke. The old woman had lengthened the bed of the fire so that a pocket of warm air lay between the flames and the rock. The flames of the fire and the smoke were a wall that interrupted any attempt of the light wind to penetrate the overhang. Mal lay on the earth in this pocket. He was curled up, grey against the brown, his eyes were shut and his mouth was open. He was breathing so quickly and shallowly that his chest seemed to beat like a heart. His bones showed plainly and his flesh was like fat that the fire was melting. Nil, the new one and Ha were just moving away down to the forest as Lok came in sight. They ate as they went and Ha waved a congratulatory hand at Lok. The old woman was standing by the fire, picking at the stomach which Fa had left with her.

Fa and Lok dropped down to the terrace and ran to the fire. As he piled his meat on the scattered rocks Lok shouted across the flames to Mal.

"Mal! Mal! We have meat!"

Mal opened his eyes and got himself on one elbow. He looked across the fire at the swinging stomach and panted a grin at Lok. Then he turned to the old woman. She smiled at him and began to beat the free hand on her thigh.

"That is good, Mal. That is strength."

Liku was jumping up and down beside her.

"I ate meat. And little Oa ate meat. I frightened the beaks away, Mal."

Mal was grinning round at them and panting.

"Then after all, Mal saw a good picture."

48

Lok tore out a scrap of meat and chewed it. He began to laugh, staggering along the terrace in mime of the load as he had mimed the night before. He spoke indistinctly with his mouth full.

"And Lok saw a true picture. Honey for Liku and the little Oa. And armfuls of meat that a cat had killed."

They laughed with him and beat their thighs. Mal lay back, the grin faded from his face and he was silent, concentrating on his pulsing breath. Fa and the old woman sorted the meat and laid some aside on shelves of rock or in the recesses. Liku took another piece of liver and edged round the fire into the pocket where Mal lay. Then the old woman lowered the stomach gently on to a rock, untwisted the mouth and began to poke about inside.

"Bring earth."

Fa and Lok went through the entry to the terrace where rocks and bushes sloped down to the forest. They tore out lumps of coarse grass with the earth still hanging to them and brought the loads back to the old woman. She took the stomach and laid it on the ground. She scraped up fire ash with a flat stone. Lok squatted on the terrace and began to break up earth with a stick. As he worked he talked.

"Ha and Nil have brought many days' wood back. Fa and Lok have brought many days' food back. And soon the warm days will be here."

As he collected the dry, broken earth, Fa wetted it with water from the river. She carried it to the old woman who plastered it round the stomach. Then she quickly raked out the hottest ashes of the fire and piled them round the plastered earth. The ashes lay thick and the

49

air over them shivered with heat. Fa brought more earth and sods. The old woman built these into a pile round the ashes and shut them in. Lok stopped work and stood, looking down at the food. He could see the puckered mouth of the stomach and plastered earth, then the sods. Fa nudged him aside, bent down and poured water from her cupped hands into the mouth. The old woman watched critically as Fa ran back and forth. Again and again she came from the sliding river until the surface of the water in the stomach lay level with the mouth, flat and scummy. Little bubbles bulged out of the scum, wandered and blipped out. The grass on the sods that covered the red-hot ashes began to curl. It writhed and began to blacken and smoulder. Little flames popped out of the earth and ran about in the grass or moved in balls of consuming yellow from the base of a stem to the end. Lok stepped back and reached for scraps of earth. As he poured them over the burning sods he talked to the old woman.

"It is easy to keep the fire in. The flames will not crawl away. There is nothing here for them to eat."

The old woman smiled wisely at him, saying nothing, and this made him feel silly. He tore a strip of muscle from a flabby haunch and wandered down the terrace. The sun was over the gap through the mountains and he adjusted himself without thinking to the fact that now the end part of the day was coming. Part of the day had gone so quickly that he felt he had lost something. He began to picture confusedly the overhang when he and Fa had not been in it. Mal and the old woman had waited, she pondering Mal's sickness, Mal panting, waiting for Ha with wood and Lok with food. Suddenly he understood that Mal had not been certain that they would find food. Yet Mal was wise. Though Lok felt important again at the thought of the meat, yet the knowledge that Mal had not been certain was like a cold wind. Then the knowledge, so nearly like thinking, made a tiredness in his head and he shook it off, returning to be the comfortable and happy Lok whose betters told him what to do and looked after him. He remembered the old woman, so close to Oa, knowing so indescribably much, the doorkeeper to whom all secrets were open. He felt awed and happy and witless again.

Fa was sitting by the fire toasting scraps of meat on a twig. The scraps spat and trickled as the twig burned and she stung her fingers every time she took meat off to eat. The old woman was pouring water from her hands over Mal's face. Liku sat with her back against the rock and the little Oa was on her shoulder. Liku was eating slowly now, her legs were stretched out straight in front of her and her belly was beautifully round. The old woman came back and squatted by Fa and watched the wisp of steam that rose from the bubbles in the stomach. She snatched a floating titbit, juggled with it and popped it in her mouth.

The people were silent. Life was fulfilled, there was no need to look farther for food, to-morrow was secure and the day after that so remote that no one would bother to think of it. Life was exquisitely allayed hunger. Soon Mal would eat of the soft brain. The strength and fleetness of the doe would begin to grow in him. With the wonder of this gift present in their minds they felt no need for speech. They sank then into a settled silence that might have been mistaken for abstracted melancholy, were it

51

not for the steady movement of the muscles that ran up from their jaws and moved the curls gently on the sides of their vaulted heads.

Liku's head nodded and the little Oa fell off her shoulder. The bubbles rose busily in the mouth of the stomach, slipped to the edge and a cloud of steam puffed upwards to be sucked sideways into the rising air of the bigger fire. Fa took a twig, dipped it in the seething mess, tasted the end and turned to the old woman.

"Soon."

The old woman tasted too.

"Mal must drink of the hot water. There is strength in the water from the meat."

Fa was frowning at the stomach. She put her right hand flat on top of her head.

"I have a picture."

She scrambled out of the overhang and pointed back towards the forest and the sea.

"I am by the sea and I have a picture. This is a picture of a picture. I am——" She screwed up her face and scowled—"thinking." She came back and squatted by the old woman. She rocked to and fro a little. The old woman rested the knuckles of one hand on the earth and scratched under her lip with the other. Fa went on speaking. "I have a picture of the people emptying the shells by the sea. Lok is shaking bad water out of a shell."

Lok began to chatter but Fa stopped him.

"—There is Liku and Nil——" She paused, frustrated by the vivid detail of her picture, not knowing how to extract from it the significance she felt was there. Lok laughed. Fa brushed at him as at a fly.

"—water out of a shell."

She looked at the old woman hopefully. She sighed, and started again.

"Liku is in the forest——"

Lok pointed, laughing, to Liku who lay against a rock, sleeping. Fa struck at him this time as though she had a baby on her back.

"It is a picture. Liku is coming through the forest. She carries the little Oa——"

She was gazing earnestly at the old woman. Then Lok saw the strain go out of her face and knew that they were sharing a picture. It came to him too, a meaningless jumble of shells and Liku and water, and the overhang. He began to speak.

"There are no shells by the mountains. Only shells of the little snail people. They are caves for them."

The old woman was leaning towards Fa. Then she swayed back, lifted both hands off the earth and poised on her skinny hams. Slowly, deliberately, her face changed to that face she would make suddenly if Liku strayed too near the flaunting colours of the poison berry. Fa shrank before her and put her hands up to her face. The old woman spoke.

"That is a new thing."

She left Fa who bowed her face over the stomach and began to stir it with a twig.

The old woman laid a hand on Mal's foot and shook it gently. Mal opened his eyes but did not move. There was a tiny patch of dark saliva-stained earth on the ground by his mouth. The sunlight slanted into the overhang from the night side of the gap and lit him brightly so that shadows stretched from him to the other end of the fire. The old woman put her mouth close to his head.

"Eat, Mal."

Mal got up on one elbow, panting.

"Water!"

Lok ran down to the river and came back with water in his hands, and Mal sucked it up. Then Fa knelt on the other side and let him lean against her while the old woman dipped a stick in the broth more times than there were fingers in the whole world and put it to his mouth. There was hardly time between his breathings for him to swallow. At last he began to turn his head from side to side, avoiding the stick. Lok brought him water. Fa and the old woman laid him carefully on his side. He withdrew from them. They could see how private his thought was and how trapped. The old woman stood by the fire looking down at him. They could see that something of his privacy had reached her and lay in her face like a cloud. Fa broke away from them and ran down to the river. Lok read her lips.

"Nil?"

He went after her into the evening light and together they peered along the cliff over the river. Neither Nil nor Ha was to be seen and the forest beyond the fall was already darkening.

"They are carrying too much wood."

Fa made an agreeing noise.

"But they will bring big wood up the slope. Ha has many pictures. To carry wood on the cliff is bad."

Then they knew that the old woman was looking at them and thinking that she was the only one who understood about Mal. They came back to share the cloud in her face. The child Liku was asleep against the rock, her

54

round belly glowing in the firelight. Mal had not even moved a finger but his eyes were still open. Suddenly the sunlight was level. There was a flapping noise from the cliff over the river and then the scrape of someone edging round the corner. Nil hurried to them along the terrace, her hands empty. She cried her words out.

"Where is Ha?"

Lok gaped at her stupidly.

"He is carrying wood with Nil and the new one."

Nil jerked at them. All at once she was shivering, though she stood within an arm's-length of the fire. Then she began talking quickly to the old woman.

"Ha is not with Nil. See!"

She ran round on the terrace demonstrating its emptiness. She came back. She peered into the overhang, caught up a piece of meat and began to tear at it. The new one woke under her hair and put out his head. After a moment she took the meat from her mouth and looked closely at each of them in turn.

"Where is Ha?"

The old woman pressed her hands on her head, considered this fresh problem for a moment and gave up. She crouched by the stomach and began to fish out meat.

"Ha was gathering wood with you."

Nil became violent.

"No! No! No!"

She bounced up and down on her feet. Her breasts bobbed and milk showed in the nipples. The new one sniffed and scrambled over her shoulder. She held him fiercely with both hands so that he mewed before he sucked. She crouched on the rock and gathered them urgently with her eyes.

55

"See the picture. We bring wood into a pile. Where the big dead tree is. In the open space. We talk about the doe that Fa and Lok have brought. We laugh together."

She looked across the fire and stretched out a hand.

"Mal!"

His eyes turned towards her. He went on panting. Nil talked at him, while the new one sucked at her breast and behind her the sunlight left the water.

"Then Ha goes toward the river to drink and I stay by the wood." She looked as Fa had looked when the details of the picture were too much for her. "Also he goes to ease himself. And I stay by the wood. But he cries out: 'Nil!' When I stand up"—she was miming—"I see Ha running up towards the cliff. He is running after something. He looks back and he is glad and then he is frightened and glad—so! Then I cannot see him any more." They followed her gaze up a cliff and could not see him any more. "I wait and wait. Then I go to the cliff for Ha and to come back for the wood. There is no sun on the cliff."

Her hair bristled and her teeth showed.

"There is a smell on the cliff. Two. Ha and another. Not Lok. Not Fa. Not Liku. Not Mal. Not her. Not Nil. There is another smell of a nobody. Going up the cliff and coming back. But the smell of Ha stops. There is Ha going up the cliff over the weed-tails when the sun has gone down; and then nothing."

The old woman began to move the sods from the stomach. She spoke over her shoulder.

"That is a picture in a dream. There is no other."

Nil started again in anguish.

"Not Lok. Not Mal——" She went sniffing over the

56

rock, found herself too near the corner that gave on to the cliff and came bristling back. "There is the end of the Ha scent. Mal——!"

The others considered this picture gravely. The old woman opened the steaming bag. Nil jumped over the fire and knelt by Mal. She touched his cheek.

"Mal! Do you hear?"

Mal answered her between gasps.

"I hear."

The old woman held out meat to Nil who took it without eating. She waited for Mal to speak again, but the old woman spoke for him.

"Mal is very sick. Ha has many pictures. Eat now and be happy."

Nil screamed at her so fiercely that the people stopped eating too.

"There is no Ha. The Ha scent has ended."

For a moment no one moved. Then the people turned and looked down at Mal. With much labour he raised his body, and balanced himself on his hams. The old woman opened her mouth to speak, then shut it. Mal put his hands flat on top of his head. This made his balance even more difficult. He began to jerk.

"Ha went to the cliffs."

He coughed and lost what breath he had. They waited while the fast rhythm of his breath evened.

"There is the scent of another."

He pulled down with both hands. His body began to quiver. One leg shot out and the heel stayed him from a fall. The others waited, red in the sunset and firelight, while the steam from the broth poured up with the reek to be hidden by darkness.

"There is the scent of others."

For a moment he held his breath. Then they saw the wasted muscles of his body relax and he fell sideways as if he did not care how he struck himself against the earth. They saw him whisper.

"I cannot see this picture."

Even Lok was silent. The old woman went to the recesses and fetched wood as if she were walking in her sleep. She did things by touch and her eyes looked beyond the people. Because they could not see what she saw they stood still and meditated formlessly the picture of no Ha. But Ha was with them. They knew his every inch and expression, his individual scent, his wise and silent face. His thorn bush lay against the rock, part of the shaft water-smooth from his hot grip. The accustomed rock waited for him, there before them was the worn mark of his body on the earth. All these things came together in Lok. They made his heart swell, gave him strength as if he might will Ha to them out of the air.

Suddenly Nil spoke.

"Ha is gone."

FOUR

Astonished, Lok watched the water run out of her eyes. It lingered at the rim of her eye-hollows, then fell in great drops on her mouth and the new one. She ran down to the river and howled into the night. He saw the drops from Fa's eyes flash in the fire-light too and then she was with Nil, howling at the river. The feeling that Ha was still present by his many evidences grew so strong in Lok that it overwhelmed him. He ran after them, seized Nil by the wrist and swung her round.

"No!"

She was clutching the new one so fiercely that he was whimpering. The water still dropped from her face. She shut her eyes and opened her mouth and howled again high and long. Lok shook her in rage.

"Ha is not gone! See——"

He ran back to the overhang and pointed to the thorn bush, the rock and the print in the soil. Ha was every-where. Lok chattered at the old woman.

"I have a picture of Ha. I will find him. How could Ha meet another? There is no other in the world——"

Fa began to talk eagerly. Nil was sniffing noisily and listening.

"If there is another then Ha has gone with him. Let Lok and Fa go——"

The old woman made a gesture that stopped her.

"Mal is very sick and Ha has gone." She looked at each of them in turn. "Now there is only Lok."

"I will find him."

"—and Lok has many words and no pictures. There is no hope in Mal. Therefore let me speak."

She squatted down ceremoniously by the steaming bag. Lok caught her eye and the pictures went from his head. The old woman began to speak with authority as Mal would have done were he not sick.

"Without help Mal will die. Fa must take a present to the ice women and speak for him to Oa."

Fa squatted by her.

"What other man can this be? Is one alive who was dead? Is one come back from Oa's belly as it may be my baby that died in the cave by the sea?"

Nil sniffed again.

"Let Lok go and find him."

The old woman rebuked her.

"A woman for Oa and a man for the pictures in his head. Let Lok speak."

Lok found himself laughing foolishly. He was at the head of the procession, not capering happily at the other end with Liku. The attention of the three women beat at him. He looked down and scratched one foot with the other. He shuffled round until his back was to them.

"Speak, Lok!"

He tried to fix his eyes on some point in the shadows that would draw him away and enable him to forget them. Half-seeing, he glimpsed the thorn bush leant against the rock. All at once the Ha-ness of Ha was with him in the overhang. An extreme excitement filled him. He began to chatter.

"Ha has a mark here under the eye where the stick burned him. He smells—so! He speaks. There is the little patch of hair over his big toe——"

He jumped round.

"Ha has found another. See! Ha falls from the cliff— that is a picture. Then the other comes running. He cries out to Mal: 'Ha has fallen in the water!'"

Fa peered closely in his face.

"The other did not come."

The old woman had her by the wrist.

"Then Ha did not fall. Go quickly, Lok. Find Ha and the other."

Fa frowned.

"Does the other know Mal?"

Lok laughed again.

"Everyone knows Mal!"

Fa made a quick gesture at him, bidding him be silent. She put her fingers to her teeth and tugged at them. Nil was looking at each of them in turn not understanding what they said. Fa whipped the fingers out of her mouth and pointed one in the old woman's face.

"Here is a picture. Someone is—other. Not one of the people. He says to Ha: 'Come! Here is more food than I can eat.' Then Ha says——"

Her voice faded away. Nil began to whimper.

"Where is Ha?"

The old woman answered her.

"He has gone with the other man."

Lok seized Nil and shook her a little.

"They have changed words or shared a picture. Ha

61

will tell us and I will go after him." He looked round at them. "People understand each other."

The people considered this and shook their heads in agreement.

Liku woke up and smiled round at them. The old woman began to busy herself in the overhang. She and Fa muttered together, they compared pieces of meat, hefted bones and came back to the stomach to argue. Nil sat by it, tearful and eating with a mechanical and listless persistence. The new one crawled slowly over her shoulder. He balanced for a moment, looked at the fire and then inserted himself under her hair. Then the old woman looked secretly at Lok so that even the mixed picture of Ha and another went out of his head and he stood first on one foot then the other. Liku came to the stomach and burnt her fingers. The old woman went on looking and at last Nil sniffed and spoke to him.

"Have you a picture of Ha? A true picture?"

The old woman picked up his thorn bush and handed it to him. She was mixed fire and moonlight and Lok's feet carried him out of the overhang.

"I have a true picture."

Fa gave him food quickly from the stomach, food so hot that he had to juggle with it. He looked doubtfully at them and wandered to the corner. Out of the firelight everything was black and silver, black island, rocks and trees carved cleanly out of the sky and silver river with a flashing light rippling back and forth along the lip of the fall. All at once the night was very lonely and the picture of Ha would not come back into his head. He glanced at the overhang to find the picture. It was a flickering hollow in the cliff at the top of the terrace with a curving line of black at the bottom where the earth rose and hid the fire. He could see Fa and the old woman crouched together and they held a bundle of meat between them. He edged out of sight round the corner and the sound of the fall swelled to meet him. He grounded his thorn bush and squatted to eat his food. It was tender and hot and good. He no longer felt the desperate pain of hunger but only zest, so that the food could be enjoyed and not bolted. He held it close to his face and inspected the pallid surface where the moonlight lay more sleekly than on the water. He forgot the overhang and Ha. He became Lok's belly. As he sat above the thunderous fall with the dim expanses of water-riddled forest before him his face shone with grease and serene happiness. To-night was colder than last night though he made no comparisons. There was a diamond glitter in the mist of the fall that was due only to the brightness of the moon but it looked like ice. The wind had died away and the only beings that moved were the hanging ferns that were tugged by the water. He watched the island without seeing it and attended to the sweetness over his tongue, the full clucking swallow and the tightness of his skin.

At last the meat was finished. He cleaned his face with his hands and his teeth with one of the points from the thorn bush. He remembered Ha again and the overhang and the old woman and stood up quickly. He began to use his nose consciously, crouching sideways and sniffing at the rock. The smells were very complex and his nose did not seem to be clever. He knew why that was and lowered himself head downward till he felt the water with

63

his lips. He drank then cleared out his mouth. He clambered back and crouched on the worn rock. Rain had smoothed it but the close passage by the corner was worn down by the innumerable passings of men like himself. He stood for a while over the monstrous booming of the fall and attended to his nose. The scents were a pattern in space and time. Here, by his shoulder, was the freshest scent of Nil's hand on the rock. Below it was a company of smells, smells of the people as they had passed this way yesterday, smells of sweat and milk and the sour smell of Mal in his pain. Lok sorted and discarded these and settled on the last smell of Ha. Each smell was accompanied by a picture more vivid than memory, a sort of living but qualified presence, so that now Ha was alive again. He settled the picture of Ha in his head, intending to keep it there so that he would not forget.

He was standing crouched, holding the thorn bush in one hand. Then slowly he lifted it, took it with both hands. The knuckles paled and he took a cautious step back. There was something else. It was not noticeable when all the people were considered together, but sort and eliminate them and it remained, a smell without a picture. Now that he noticed, it was heavy by the corner. Someone had stood there, his hand on the rock, leaning, peering round at the terrace and the overhang. Without thinking, Lok understood the blank amazement in Nil's face. He began to move forward along the cliff, slowly at first, then running till he was flitting across the rock-face. A confusion of pictures flickered through his head as he ran: here was Nil, bewildered, frightened, here the other, here came Ha, moving fast——

Lok turned and ran back. On that platform where he

himself had so inexplicably fallen, the scent of Ha broke off as if the cliff ended.

Lok leaned out and looked down. He could see the weed-tails waving under the brilliance of the river. He felt the sounds of mourning about to break from his throat and clapped a hand over his mouth. The weed-tails waved, the river rolled a tide of twisted silver along the dark shore of the island. There came to him a picture of Ha struggling in the water, borne by the current towards the sea. Lok began to track along the rock, following the scent of Ha and the other down towards the forest. He passed the bushes where Ha had found berries for Liku, withered berries, and he still lived there, caught in the bushes. The palm of his hand had pulled along the twigs, forcing the berries off them. He was alive in Lok's head, but backwards, moving through time towards their spring coming from the sea. Lok bounded down the slope between the rocks and under the trees of the forest. The moon that shone so brightly on the river was broken here by the high buds and motionless branches. The tree trunks made great bars of darkness but when he moved between them the moon dropped a net of light over him. Here was Ha and his excitement. Here he went towards the river. There, by the abandoned pile of wood was the patch where Nil had waited patiently till her feet made prints that were black now in a splash of light. Here she had followed Ha, puzzled, worried. The mingling tracks ran back up the rocks towards the cliff.

Lok remembered Ha in the river. He began to run, keeping as near the bank as he could. He came to the open patch where the dead tree stood and ran down to the water. Bushes grew out of the water and hung over it. The branches trailing in the current made it visible by combing moon out of the blackness. Lok began to call out.

"Ha! Where are you."

The river did not answer. Lok called again and waited while the picture of Ha became dim and disappeared so that he understood that Ha had gone. Then there came a cry from the island. Lok shouted again and jumped up and down. But as he jumped he began to feel that Ha's voice had not called. This was a different voice; not the voice of the people. It was the voice of other. Suddenly he was filled with excitement. It was of desperate importance that he should see this man whom he smelt and heard. He ran round the clearing, aimlessly, crying out at the top of his voice. Then the smell of other came to him from the damp earth and he followed it away from the river towards the slope up to the mountain. He followed it, bent, flickering under the moon. The smell curved away from the river under the trees and came to the tumbled rocks and bushes. Here was possible danger, cats or wolves or even the great foxes, red as Lok himself, that the spring hunger made savage. But the trail of other was simple and not even crossed by an animal's scent. It kept away from the path up to the overhang, preferring for choice the beds of gullies rather than the steeper rocks at the side. The other had paused here and there, had paused unaccountably long, his feet turned back. Once where the going was smooth and steep the other had walked backwards for more steps than there were fingers in a hand. He had turned again and started to run up the gully, and his feet had kicked up earth, or rather

66

forced it out wherever they had fallen on a patch. He had paused again, climbed the side of the gully, lain for a while at the lip. There built up in Lok's head a picture of the man, not by reasoned deduction but because in every place the scent told him—do this! As the smell of cat would evoke in him a cat-stealth of avoidance and a cat-snarl; as the sight of Mal tottering up the slope had made the people parody him, so now the scent turned Lok into the thing that had gone before him. He was beginning to know the other without understanding how it was that he knew. Lok-other crouched at the lip of the cliff and stared across the rocks of the mountain. He threw himself forward and was running with legs and back bent. He threw himself into the shadow of a rock, snarling and waiting. He moved cautiously forward, he got down on hands and knees, crawled forward slowly and looked over the edge of the cliff into the river-filled gap.

He was looking down at the overhang. The rock projected above it and he could not see any of the people; but from under the rock a semicircle of ruddy light danced on the terrace, diminishing outward till it was indistinguishable from the moonlight. A little smoke was pouring up and drifting away through the gap. Lok-other began to edge down the rock from ledge to ledge. As he approached the overhang itself he went even more slowly and pressed his body flat against the rock. He pushed himself forward, leaned out and looked down. At once his eye was dazzled by a tongue of flame from the fire; he was Lok again, at home with the people, and the other was gone. Lok stayed where he was, looking blankly at the earth and stones and the sane, comfortable terrace. Fa spoke just beneath him. They were strange words and meant nothing to him. Fa appeared, carrying a bundle and trotted away along the terrace to the dizzy suggestion of a path that led up to the ice women. The old woman came out, looked after her, then turned back under the rock. Lok heard wood scrape, then a shower of sparks floated upwards past his face and the firelight on the terrace spread more widely and began to dance.

Lok sat back and stood up slowly. His head was empty. He had no pictures. Along the terrace Fa had left the flat rock and earth and had started to climb. The old woman came out of the overhang, ran down to the river and came back with a double handful of water. She was so close that Lok could see the drops that fell from her fingers and the twin fires reflected in her eyes. She passed under the rock and he knew that she had not seen him. All at once Lok was frightened because she had not seen him. The old woman knew so much; yet she had not seen him. He was cut off and no longer one of the people; as though his communion with the other had changed him he was different from them and they could not see him. He had no words to formulate these thoughts but he felt his difference and invisibility as a cold wind that blew on his skin. The other had tugged at the strings that bound him to Fa and Mal and Liku and the rest of the people. The strings were not the ornament of life but its substance. If they broke, a man would die. All at once he was hungry for someone's eyes to meet his and recognize him. He turned to run along the ledges and drop down to the overhang; but here was the scent of other again. No longer viciously a part of Lok, its strangeness and power drew him. He followed the scent along the ledges that lay above the terrace until it led to the place where the terrace petered out by the water and the way to the ice women lay above him.

The scattered rocks of the island swept in here and broke up the current not the length of many men away. The scent went down to the water and Lok went with it. He stood, shivering slightly at the loneliness of the water and looking at the nearer rock. A picture began to form in his head of the leap that had cleared this gap to land the other on the rock, and then, leap by leap over the deadly water to the dark island. The moon was caught round the rocks and they were outlined. As he watched, one of the farther rocks began to change shape. At one side a small bump elongated then disappeared quickly. The top of the rock swelled, the hump fined off at the base and elongated again then halved its height. Then it was gone.

Lok stood and let the pictures come and go in his head. One was a picture of a cave bear that he had once seen rear itself out of the rock and heard roar like the sea. Lok did not know much more about the bear than that because after the bear had roared the people had run for most of a day. This thing, this black changing shape, had something of the bear's slow movement in it. He screwed up his eyes and peered at the rock to see if it would change again. There was a single birch tree that overtopped the other trees on the island, and was now picked out against the moon-drenched sky. It was very thick at the base, unduly thick, and as Lok watched, impossibly thick. The blob of darkness seemed to coagulate round the stem like a drop of blood on a stick. It lengthened, thickened again, lengthened. It moved up the birch tree with sloth-like deliberation, it hung in the air high above the island

and the fall. It made no noise and at last hung motionless. Lok cried out at the top of his voice; but either the creature was deaf or the ponderous fall erased the words that he said.

"Where is Ha?"

The creature did not move. A little wind pushed through the gap and the top of the birch swayed, its arc made wide and sedate by the black weight that clung to it. The hair rose on Lok's body and some of the unease of the mountainside returned to him. He felt the need for the protection of human beings, yet memory of the old woman who had not seen him kept him from the over-hang. He stayed therefore while the lump swung down the birch tree and vanished into the anonymous shadows that made up this part of the island. Then the lump appeared again, changing shape over the farthest rock. In a panic Lok scrambled in the moonlight at the side of the mountain. Before he could see a clear picture in his head he was scrambling up the suggestion of a track where Fa had gone. He paused when he was as high above the gap-water as a tree is tall and looked down. The creature was visible for an instant as it leapt from rock to rock. Lok shivered and set himself to climb.

This rock did not lean back; it stretched up, becoming steeper as it went and in places sheer. He came to a kind of slit in the cliff and water was falling from it to slide along and dive into the gap. This water was so cold that it bit him when a drop splashed on his face. He could smell Fa and meat on the rock and climbed into the slit. This led straight upward, with a slice of moony sky at the top. The rock was slippery with water and sought to be rid of him. The scent of Fa led him on. When he reached the place where the sky was, he found that the slit became a wide gully that appeared to lead straight into the mountain. He looked down and the river was thin in the gap and everything changed in shape. He wanted Fa more than ever and ducked into the gully. Behind him and across the gap the mountains were horns of ice that shone. He could hear Fa only a little way in front of him and cried out. She came back fast down the gully, leaping on the stones where the water clattered. Boulders grated by her feet and the noise rebounded from the cliffs so that she sounded like a whole party of people. Then she was close to him, her face convulsed with rage and fear.

"Be silent!"

Lok did not hear. He was babbling.

"I have seen the other. Ha fell in the river. The other came and watched the overhang."

Fa seized him by the arm. The bundle was clutched against her breast.

"Be silent! Oa will let the ice women hear and they will fall!"

"Let me stay with you!"

"You are a man. There is terror. Go back!"

"I will not see or hear. I will stay behind you. Let me come."

The drone of the fall had diminished to a sigh like the sound of the sea at a great distance, but in bad weather. Their words had flown away from them like a flock of birds that circled and multiplied mysteriously. The cliffs of the deep gully were singing. Fa clapped her hand over his mouth and they stood so while the birds flew farther and farther away and there was no sound but the water by their feet and the sighing of the fall. Fa turned and began to climb the gully and Lok hastened after her. She stopped and motioned him back fiercely but when she went on he followed. Then Fa stopped again, and ran to and fro between the cliffs making silent mouths at Lok and showing her teeth but he would not leave her. The way back led to the Lok-other who had been unutterably alone. At last she gave up and ignored him. She padded up the gully and Lok followed her, his teeth rattling with the cold.

For here at last there was no water by their feet. There were instead, congealed trunks of ice that were fixed solidly against the cliff; and under the unsunned side of every stone lay a bank of snow. He felt all the misery of winter again and the terror of the ice women so that he followed Fa close as though she were a warm fire. The sky was a narrow strip above him, a freezing sky, that was pricked all over with stars and dashed with strokes of cloud that trapped the moonlight. He could see now that the ice clung to the sides of the gully like ivy, broad below and dividing higher up into a thousand branches and tendrils and the leaves were a glittering white. There was ice under his feet so that they burned and then were numbed. Soon he was using his hands as well and they were numbed like his feet. Fa's rump bobbed in front of him and he followed. The gully widened and more light spilled in and he could see that they were facing a sheer wall of rock. Down the left side there was a line of deepest black. Fa crept towards this line and vanished into it. Lok followed her. He was in an entry so narrow that he could touch both sides with his elbows. Then he was through.

Light hit him. He ducked and brought both hands up to his eyes. Blinking, looking down, he could see stones that flashed, lumps of ice and deep blue shadows. He could see Fa's feet in front of him, whitened, dusted with glitter and her shadow changing shape over the ice and stones. He began to look forward at eye-level and he saw the clouds of their breathing hanging round them like the spray clouds of the fall. He stayed where he was and Fa dimmed into her own breath.

The place was huge and open. It was walled with rock; and everywhere the ice ivy-plants reached upwards until they were spread out high above his head on the rock. Where they met the floor of the sanctuary they swelled till they were like the boles of old oaks. Their high branches vanished into caverns of ice. Lok stood back and looked up at Fa who had gone higher towards the other end of the sanctuary. She crouched on the stones and lifted up the parcel of meat. There was no sound, not even the noise of the fall.

Fa began to speak in little more than a whisper. At first he could hear individual words, "Oa" and "Mal": but walls rejected the words so that they bounded back and were thrown again. "Oa" said the wall and the great ivy, and the wall behind Lok sang "Oa Oa Oa". They ceased to utter the separate words and sang "O" and "A" at the same moment. The sound rose like water in a tidal pool, smoothed like water, became a ringing "A" that beat on him, drowned him. "Sick, sick," said the wall at the end of the sanctuary; "Mal" said the rocks behind him, and the air sang with the interminable and rising tide of "Oa". The hair lifted on his skin. He made with his mouth as if to say "Oa". He looked up, and saw the ice women. The caverns where the ivy branches led were their loins. Their thighs and bellies rose out of the cliff above. They impended so that the sky was smaller than the floor of the sanctuary. Body linked with body they leaned out, arching over and their pointed heads flashed in the light of the moon. He saw that their loins were like caverns, blue and terrible. They were detached from the rock and the ivy was their water, seeping down between the rock and the ice. The pool of sound had risen to their knees.

"Aaaa" sang the cliff, "Aaaa——"

Lok was lying with his face against ice. Though the frost twinkled on his hair sweat had burst through his skin. He could feel the ravine moving sideways. Fa was shaking his arm.

"Come!"

His belly felt as though he had eaten grass and would be sick. He could see nothing but green lights that moved with merciless persistence through a void of blackness. The sound of the sanctuary had entered his head and was living there like the sound of the sea in a shell. Fa's lips moved against his ear.

"Before they see you."

He remembered the ice women. He kept his eyes on the ground lest he should see the awful light and began to crawl away. His body was a dead thing and he could not make it work. He stumbled after Fa and then they were through the crack in the wall and the gully led down in front of them and another crack was the new arrangement of the gap. He fled past Fa and began to fight his way downward. He fell and rolled, stumbled, leapt clumsily among snow and stones. Then he stopped, weak and shaken and whimpering like Nil. Fa came to him. She put her arm round him and he leaned, looking down at the thread-like water of the gap. Fa spoke softly in his ear.

"It is too much Oa for a man."

He turned inward and got his head between her breasts.

"I was afraid."

For a time they were silent. But the cold was in them and their bodies shuddered apart.

In less panic but still crippled by the cold they began to feel their way down the steepening slope where the sound of the fall rose to meet them. This brought pictures of the overhang to Lok. He began to explain to Fa.

"The other is on the island. He is a mighty leaper. He was on the mountain. He came to the overhang and looked down."

"Where is Ha?"

"He fell into the water."

She left a cloud of breath behind her and he heard her voice out of it.

"No man falls in water. Ha is on the island."

For a while she was silent. Lok thought as best he could of Ha leaping the gap across to the rock. He could not see this picture. Fa spoke again.

"The other must be a woman."

"He smells of man."

"Then there must be another woman. Can a man come out of a man's belly? Perhaps there was a woman and then a woman and then a woman. By herself."

Lok digested this. As long as there was a woman there was life. But what use was a man save for smelling things out and having pictures? Confirmed in his humility he

75

did not like to tell Fa that he had seen the other or that he had seen the old woman and known himself invisible. Presently even pictures and the thought of speech went from his head for they had reached the vertical part of the trail. They clambered down in silence and the roar of water came at them. Only when they were on the terrace and trotting towards the overhang did he remember that he had set out to find Ha and was coming back without him. As if the terror of the sanctuary was pursuing them the two people broke into a run.

But Mal was not the new man they expected. He lay collapsed and his breathing was so shallow that his chest hardly moved. They could see that his face was olive dark and shone with sweat. The old woman had kept the fire blazing and Liku had moved outside it. She was eating more liver, slowly and gravely, and watching Mal. The two women were crouched, one on either side of him, Nil bent and brushing the sweat off his forehead with her hair. There seemed no place in the underhang for Lok's news of the other. When she heard them, Nil looked up, saw no Ha and bent to dry the old man's forehead again. The old woman patted his shoulder.

"Be well and strong, old man. Fa has taken an offering to Oa for you."

At that, Lok remembered his terror beneath the ice women. He opened his mouth to chatter but Fa had shared his picture and she clapped her hand across his lips. The old woman did not notice. She took another morsel from the steaming bag.

"Sit up now and eat."

Lok spoke to him.

"Ha is gone. There are other people in the world."

76

Nil stood up and Lok knew that she was going to mourn but the old woman spoke as Fa had done.

"Be silent!"

She and Fa lifted Mal carefully until he was sitting, leaning back in their arms, his head rolling on Fa's breast. The old woman placed the morsel between his lips but they mumbled it out again. He was speaking.

"Do not open my head and my bones. You would only taste weakness."

Lok glanced round at each of the women, his mouth open. An involuntary laugh came from it. Then he chattered at Mal.

"But there is other. And Ha has gone."

The old woman looked up.

"Fetch water."

Lok ran down to the river and brought back two handfuls. He dripped it slowly over Mal's face. The new one appeared, yawning on Nil's shoulder, clambered over and began to suck. They could see that Mal was trying to speak again.

"Put me in the warm earth by the fire."

In the noise of the waterfall there came a great silence. Even Liku ceased to eat and stood staring. The women did not move, but kept their eyes on Mal's face. The silence filled Lok, turned to water that stood suddenly in his eyes. Then Fa and the old woman laid Mal gently on his side. They pushed the great gaunt bones of his knees against his chest, tucked in his feet, lifted his head off the earth and put his two hands under it. Mal was very close to the fire and his eyes looked into the flames. The hair on his brows began to crinkle but he did not seem to notice. The old woman took a splinter of wood and drew

77

a line in the earth round his body. Then they lifted him to one side with the same solemn quiet.

The old woman chose a flat stone and gave it to Lok. "Dig!"

The moon was through to the sunset side of the gap, but its light was hardly noticeable on the earth for the ruddy brilliance of the firelight. Liku began to eat again. She stole round behind the grown-ups and sat against the rock at the back of the overhang. The earth was hard and Lok had to lean his weight on the stone before he could shift any. The old woman gave him a sharp splinter of bone from the doe meat and he found he could break up the surface much more easily with this. Underneath it was softer. The top layer of earth came up like slate, but below it crumbled in his hands and he could scrape it out with the stone. So he continued as the moon moved. There came into his head the picture of a younger and stronger Mal doing this but on the other side of the hearth. The clay of the hearth was a bulging round on one side of the irregular shaped hole that he was digging. Soon he came to another hearth beneath it and then another. There was a little cliff of burnt clay. Each hearth seemed thinner than the one above it, until as the hole deepened the layers were stone hard and not much thicker than birch bark. The new one finished sucking, yawned, and scrambled down to the earth. He took hold of Mal's leg, hauled himself up, leaning forward and gazed unblinkingly and brightly at the fire. Then he dropped back, scuttled round Mal and investigated the hole. He overbalanced into it and scrambled mewing in the soft earth by Lok's hands. He extracted himself arse-upward and fled back to Nil and crouched in her lap.

78

Lok sat back with a grasp. The perspiration was running down his body. The old woman touched him on the arm.

"Dig! There is only Lok!"

Wearily he returned to the hole. He pulled out an ancient bone and flung it far into the moonlight. He heaved again on the stone, then fell forward.

"I cannot."

Then, though this was a new thing, the women took stones and dug. Liku watched them and the deepening and darkening hole and said nothing. Mal was beginning to tremble. The clay pillar of hearths narrowed as they dug. It was rooted far down in a forgotten depth of the overhang. As each clay layer appeared the earth became easier to work. They began to have difficulty in keeping the sides straight. They came on dry and scentless bones, bones so long divorced from life that they had no meaning to them and were tossed on one side, bones of the legs, rib-bones, the crushed and opened bones of a head. There were stones too, some with edges that would cut or points that would bore and these they used for a moment where they were useful but did not keep. The dug earth grew into a pyramid by the hole and little avalanches of brown grains would run back as they lifted the new earth out by the handful. There were bones scattered over the pyramid. Liku played idly with the bones of the head. Then Lok got his strength back and dug too so that the hole sank more quickly. The old woman made up the fire again and the morning was grey beyond the flames.

At last the hole was finished. The women poured more water over Mal's face. He was skin and bone now. His

79

mouth was wide as if to bite the air he could not breathe. The people knelt in a semicircle round him. The old woman gathered them with her eyes.

"When Mal was strong he found much food."

Liku squatted against the rock at the back of the overhang, holding the little Oa to her chest. The new one slept under Nil's hair. Mal's fingers were moving aimlessly and his mouth was opening and closing. Fa and the old woman lifted the upper part of his body and held his head. The old woman spoke softly in his ear.

"Oa is warm. Sleep."

The movements of his body became spasmodic. His head rolled sideways on the old woman's breast and stayed there.

Nil began to keen. The sound filled the overhang, pulsed out across the water towards the island. The old woman lowered Mal on his side and folded his knees to his chest. She and Fa lifted him and lowered him into the hole. The old woman put his hands under his face and saw that his limbs lay low. She stood up and they saw no expression in her face. She went to a shelf of rock and chose one of the haunches of meat. She knelt and put it in the hole by his face.

"Eat, Mal, when you are hungry."

She bade them follow her with her eyes. They went down to the river, leaving Liku with the little Oa. The old woman took handfuls of water and the others dipped their hands too. She came back and poured the water over Mal's face.

"Drink when you are thirsty."

One by one the people trickled water over the grey, dead face. Each repeated the words. Lok was last, and as the water fell he was filled with a great feeling for Mal. He went back and got a second gift.

"Drink, Mal, when you are thirsty."

The old woman took handfuls of earth and cast them on his head. Last of the people came Liku, timidly, and did as the eyes bid her. Then she went back to the rock. At a sign from the old woman, Lok began to sweep the pyramid of earth into the hole. It fell with a soft swishing sound and soon Mal was blurred out of shape. Lok pressed the earth down with his hands and feet. The old woman watched the shape alter and disappear expressionlessly. The earth rose and filled the hole, rose still until where Mal had been was a little mound in the overhang. There was still some left. Lok swept it away from the mound and then trampled the mound down as firmly as he could.

The old woman squatted down by the freshly stamped earth and waited till they were all looking at her.

She spoke:

"Oa has taken Mal into her belly".

FIVE

fter their silence the people ate. They began to find
that tiredness lay on them like mist. There was
a blankness of Ha and Mal in the overhang. The
fire still burned and the food was good; but a sick
weariness fell on them. One by one they curled up in the
space between the fire and the rock and fell asleep. The
old woman went to the recess and brought wood. She
built up the fire until it roared like the water. She collected what was left of the food and placed it out of
harm's reach in the recesses. Then she squatted by the
mound of earth where Mal had been and looked out over
the water.

The people did not dream very often, but while the
light of the dawn brightened over them they were beset
by a throng of phantoms from the other place. The old
woman could see out of the corner of her eye how they
were enmeshed, exalted and tormented. Nil was talking.
Lok's left hand was scrabbling up a handful of dirt.
Muttered words, inarticulate cries of pleasure and fear
were coming from them all. The old woman did nothing
but gazed steadily at a picture of her own. Birds began
to cry and the sparrows dropped down and pecked about
the terrace. Lok flung out a hand suddenly that struck
her thigh.

When the water was already glittering she stood up

and brought wood from the recesses. The fire welcomed the wood with a noisy crackle. She stood close by it, looking down.

"Now, is like when the fire flew away and ate up all the trees."

Lok's hand was too near the fire. She bent down and moved it back to his face. He rolled right over and cried out.

Lok was running. The scent of the other was pursuing him and he could not get away. It was night and the scent had paws and a cat's teeth. He was on the island where he had never been. The fall roared by on either side. He was running along the bank, knowing that presently he would drop from exhaustion and the other would have him. He fell and there was an eternity of struggle. But the strings that bound him to the people were still there. Pulled by his desperate need they were coming, walking, running easily over the water, borne inevitably by necessity. The other was gone and the people were all about him. He could not see them clearly for the darkness but knew who they were. They came in, closer and closer, not as they would come into the over-hang, recognizing home and being free of the whole space; they drove in until they were being joined to him, body to body. They shared a body as they shared a picture. Lok was safe.

Liku woke up. The little Oa had fallen from her shoulder and she took it up. She yawned, saw the old woman and said that she was hungry. The old woman went to a recess and brought her the last of the liver. The new one was playing with Nil's hair. He pulled it, swung on it and she was awake and whimpering again. Fa sat up,

Lok rolled back again and nearly went into the fire. He leapt away from it chattering. He saw the others and talked to them foolishly.

"I was asleep."

The people went down to the water, drank and eased themselves. When they came back there was the feeling of much to be said in the overhang and they left two places empty as though one day those who had sat there might come back again. Nil suckled the new one and combed out her curls with her fingers.

The old woman turned from the fire and spoke to them.

"Now there is Lok."

He looked at her blankly. Fa bent her head. The old woman came to him, took him firmly by the hand and led him to one side. Here was the Mal place. She made Lok sit down, his back against the rock, his hams in the smooth earthen dip that Mal had worn. The strangeness of this overcame Lok. He looked sideways at the water, then back at the people and laughed. There were eyes everywhere, and they waited for him. He was at the head of the procession not at the back of it, and every picture went right out of his head. The blood made his face hot and he pressed his hands over his eyes. He looked through his fingers at the women, at Liku, then down at the mound where the body of Mal was buried. He wished urgently to talk to Mal, to wait quietly before him to be told what to do. But no voice came from the mound and no picture. He grasped at the first picture that came into his head.

"I dreamed. The other was chasing me. Then we were together."

84

Nil lifted the new one on her breast.

"I dreamed. Ha lay with me and with Fa. Lok lay with Fa and with me."

She began to whimper. The old woman made a gesture that startled and silenced her.

"A man for pictures. A woman for Oa. Ha and Mal have gone. Now there is Lok."

Lok's voice came out small, like Liku's.

"To-day we shall hunt for food."

The old woman waited pitilessly. There was still food piled in the recess, though little enough was left. What people would hunt for food when they were not hungry and there was food left to eat?

Fa squatted forward. While she was speaking some of the confusion died away in Lok's head. He did not listen to Fa.

"I have a picture. The other is hunting for food and the people are hunting——"

She looked the old woman daringly in the eye.

"Then the people are hungry."

Nil rubbed her back against the rock.

"That is a bad picture."

The old woman shouted over them.

"Now there is Lok!"

Lok remembered. He took his hands from his face.

"I have seen the other. He is on the island. He jumps from rock to rock. He climbs in the trees. He is dark. He changes shape like a bear in a cave."

The people looked outward to the island. It was full of sunlight and a mist of green leaves. Lok called them back.

"And I followed his scent. He was there"—and he

pointed to the roof of the overhang so that they all looked up—"he stayed and watched us. He is like a cat and he is not like a cat. He is also like, like——"

The pictures went out of his head for a while. He scratched himself under the mouth. There were so many things to be said. He wished he could ask Mal what it was that joined a picture to a picture so that the last of many came out of the first.

"Perhaps Ha is not in the river. Perhaps he is on the island with the other. Ha was a mighty jumper."

The people looked along the terrace to the place where the detached rocks of the island swept in towards the bank. Nil pulled the new one from her breast and let him crawl on the earth. The water fell from her eyes.

"That is a good picture."

"I will speak with the other. How can he be always on the island? I will hunt for a new scent."

Fa was tapping her palm against her mouth.

"Perhaps he came out of the island. Like out of a woman. Or out of the fall."

"I do not see this picture."

Now Lok found how easy it was to speak words to others who would heed them. There need not even be a picture with the words.

"Fa will look for a scent and Nil and Liku and the new one——"

The old woman would not interrupt him. She seized a great bough instead and hurled it into the fire. Lok sprang to his feet with a cry, and then was silent. The old woman spoke for him.

"Lok will not want Liku to go. There is no man. Let Fa and Lok go. This is what Lok says."

He looked at her in bewilderment and her eyes told him nothing. He began to shake his head.

"Yes," he said, "Yes."

Fa and Lok ran together to the end of the terrace.

"Do not tell the old woman that you have seen the ice women."

"When I came down the mountain on the trail of other she did not see me."

He remembered the old woman's face. "Who can tell what she sees or does not see?"

"Do not tell her."

He tried to explain.

"I have seen the other. He and I, we crawled over the mountain-side and we stalked the people."

Fa stopped and they looked at the gap between the island rock and the terrace. She pointed.

"Could even Ha jump that?"

Lok pondered the gap. The confined waters swirled and sent a tail of glistening streaks down the river. Eddies broke out of the green surface in humps. Lok began to mime his pictures.

"With the scent of other I am other. I creep like a cat. I am frightened and greedy. I am strong." He broke out of the mime and ran rapidly past Fa, then turned and faced her. "Now I am Ha and the other. I am strong."

"I do not see this picture."

"The other is on the island——"

He spread his arms as wide as he could. He flapped them like a bird. Fa grinned and then laughed. Lok laughed too, more and more delightedly to be approved. He ran round on the terrace, quacking like a duck, and

Fa laughed at him. He was about to run flapping back to the overhang to share this joke with the people when he remembered. He skidded and stopped.

"Now there is Lok."

"Find the other, Lok, and speak to him."

This reminded him of the scent. He began to nose round on the rock. No rain had fallen and the scent was very faint. He remembered the mixture of scents on the cliff over the fall.

"Come."

They ran back along the terrace past the overhang. Liku shouted to them and held up the little Oa. Lok crept round the corner and felt the touch of Fa's body on his back.

"The log killed Mal."

He turned back to her, and twitched his ears in surprise.

"I mean the log that was not there. It killed Mal."

He opened his mouth, prepared to debate but she pushed at him.

"On."

They could not miss seeing the signs of the other immediately. His smoke was rising from the middle of the island. There were many trees on the island and some of them leaned out till their branches dipped and the people could not see the shore. There were thick bushes among the trees, growing in unvisited profusion so that the rock soil was covered thick and had as many leaves as it could hold. The smoke rose in a dense coil that spread and faded. There was no doubt about it. The other had a fire and he must use logs so thick and wet that the people themselves could never have lifted them.

Fa and Lok considered the smoke without finding any picture they could share. There was smoke on the island, there was another man on the island. There was nothing in life as a point of reference.

At last Fa turned away and Lok saw that she was shivering.

"Why?"

"I am afraid."

He thought about this.

"I shall go down to the forest. That is nearest to the smoke."

"I do not want to go."

"Return to the overhang. Now there is Lok."

Fa looked again at the island. Then suddenly she was writhing herself round the corner and was gone.

Lok flitted down the cliff through the pictures of the people until he came to the place where the forest began. Here the river was only to be seen occasionally for the bushes not only hung out over whe.e the bank had been, but the water had risen so that many bushes stood with their feet in it. Where the ground was low were incursions of water over drowning grass. The trees stood on higher ground and Lok's feet made a pattern that expressed both his horror of water and his desire to see the new man or the new people. The nearer he came to the part of the shore opposite the smoke the more his excitement grew. Now he even dared water above his ankles, shuddering and prancing through it. When he found that he could not see the river or get close to it he ground his teeth and struck to the right and floundered. There was mire under the water and the bleached points of bulbs. Normally his feet would have seized these and handed them up to him but now they were nothing but a brief firmness against his shuddering skin. There was a whole covert of bushes dimmed with buds between him and the river. He began to put his faith in armfuls of boughs which came together and sagged under his weight, so that he swayed terrifyingly forward off his feet. There was really not enough strength in the sappy branches to bear him unless he sprawled spread-eagled among buds and thorns. Then he saw that there was water under him, not a handful over brown mud but deeper water into which the stems of the bushes sank out of sight. He swayed down and the bushes began to escape from his grip; he glimpsed a shining expanse at eye-level so that he cried out and scrambled with a sort of anguished levitation back to the safe, unpleasant mire. There was no way here to the river for any people but the busy moorhens. He hurried away downstream, circling into the forest where the ground was firmer and came out in the open space by the dead tree. He went down to the little earthen cliff where the deep water came swirling in: but across the water the smoke still rose out of a mystery of trees and undergrowth. A picture came into his head of the other climbing the birch tree and peering through the gap. He hurried away along the trail where the scent of the people still hung faintly until he was by the marsh water, but the new log across it had gone. The tree on which he had swung Liku was still there on the other side of the water. He looked about him and settled on a beech tree that grew so huge he might think the clouds were really caught in its branches. He seized a bough and ran up it quickly. The bole divided and there was rainwater lying in the crutch. He went up the thicker

bough hand after foot until he could feel the grave movement of the tree itself beneath the wind and his weight.
The buds were not yet out but in their green thousands
they were an obscurity like tears in the eyes so that Lok
felt impatient with them. He swung higher still until he
was in the very crown, then began to bend and wrench
away the branches between himself and the island. Now
he looked down through a hole that altered shape every
moment as the swarming buds bowed or swung sideways.
The hole contained part of the island.

There were buds everywhere on the island too, drifts
of them like clouds of bright green smoke. They drifted
all along the shore and the larger trees beyond were like
puffs rising vertically then rolling out. The background
to all this greenness was the black of trunks and branches
and there was no earth. But there was a bright eye where
the fire blazed at the base of the real smoke and it
twinkled and winked at him as the branches moved
across it. Concentrating on the fire he could at last see
the earth near it, very brown and firmer than the earth
near this side of the river. It must be full of bulbs and
fallen nuts and grubs and fungi. There was undoubtedly
good food there for the other to eat.

The fire blinked sharply. Lok blinked back. The fire
had blinked, not because of the boughs but because
someone had moved in front of it, someone as dark as the
branches.

Lok shook the top of the beech tree.

"Hoé man!"

The fire blinked twice. Suddenly Lok understood from
these passings that there was more than one person. The
heady excitement of the scent came to him again. He

shook the top of the tree as though he would break it off.

"Hoé new people!"

A great strength entered into Lok. He could have flown across the invisible water between them. He dared a desperate acrobatic in the thin boughs of the beech top, then shouted as loudly as he could.

"New people! New people!"

Suddenly he froze in the swaying branches. The new people had heard him. He could see by the blinking of the fire and the shaking of the thick bushes that they would come into sight. The fire twinkled again, but a track among the green smoke began to twist and sway down towards the river. He could hear branches cracking. He leaned out.

Then there was nothing more. The green smoke steadied or pulsed gently under the wind. The fire twinkled.

So still was Lok that he began to hear the noise of the fall, ponderous, unending. The grip which held his mind to the new people began to loosen. Other pictures came into his head.

"New people! Where is Ha?"

A spray of green down by the water's edge quivered. Lok looked closely. He followed the suggestions of twigs down to the main stem and screwed up the skin in the hollows of his eyes. There was a forearm or perhaps an upper arm across the bough and it was dark and hairy. The spray of green quivered again and the dark arm vanished. Lok blinked the water out of his eyes. A new picture of Ha on the island came to him, Ha with a bear, Ha in danger.

"Ha! Where are you?"

92

The bushes on the other bank shook and twisted. A trail of movement showed in them, moving quickly from the bank back among the trees. The fire blinked again. Then the flames vanished and a great cloud of white smoke shot up through the green, the base thinned, disappeared, the white cloud rose slowly, turning inside out as it went. Lok leaned foolishly sideways to look round the trees and bushes. The urgency gripped him. He swung himself down the branches till he could see the next tree down river. He leapt at a branch, was on it, and moving like a red squirrel from tree to tree. Then he ran up a trunk again, tore branches away and peered down.

The roar of the fall was a little dulled now and he could see the columns of spray. They brooded over the upper end of the island so that the trees there were obscured. He let his eye run from them down the island to where the bushes had moved and the fire blinked. He could see, though not clearly, into an open space among the trees. The reek from the dead fire still hung over it, slowly dispersing. There were no people in sight but he could see where the bushes had been broken and a track of torn earth made between the shore and the open space. At the inner end of this track, tree-trunks, huge, dead things with the decay of years about them, had gathered themselves together. He inspected the logs, his mouth hanging open and a free hand pressed flat on top of his head. Why should the people bring all this food—he could see the pale fungi clear across the river—and the useless wood with it? They were people without pictures in their heads. Then he saw that there was a dirty smudge in the earth where the fire had been and logs as huge had been used to build it. Without any warning fear flooded into him, fear as complete and unreasoning as Mal's when he had seen the fire burning the forest in his dream. And because he was one of the people, tied to them with a thousand invisible strings, his fear was for the people. He began to quake. The lips writhed back from his teeth, he could not see clearly. He heard his voice crying out through a roaring noise in his ears.

"Ha! Where are you? Where are you?"

Someone thick-legged ran clumsily across the clearing and disappeared. The fire stayed dead and the bushes were combed by a breeze from down river and then were quite still.

Desperately:

"Where are you?"

Lok's ears spoke to Lok.

"?"

So concerned was he with the island that he paid no attention to his ears for a time. He clung swaying gently in the tree-top while the fall grumbled at him and the space on the island remained empty. Then he heard. There were people coming, not on the other side of the water but on this side, far off. They were coming down from the overhang, their steps careless on the stones. He could hear their speech and it made him laugh. The sounds made a picture in his head of interlacing shapes, thin, and complex, voluble and silly, not like the long curve of a hawk's cry, but tangled like line weed on the beach after a storm, muddled as water. This laugh-sound advanced through the trees towards the river. The same sort of laugh-sound began to rise on the island, so that it flitted back and forth across the water. Lok half-fell, half-scrambled down the tree and was on the trail. He ran along it through the ancient smell of the people. The laugh-sound was close by the river bank. Lok reached the place where the log had lain across water. He had to climb a tree, swing and drop down before he was on the trail again. Then among the laugh-sound on this side of the river Liku began to scream. She was not screaming in anger or in fear or in pain, but screaming with that mindless and dreadful panic she might have shown at the slow advance of a snake. Lok spurted, his hair bristling. Need to get at that screaming threw him off the trail and he floundered. The screaming tore him inside. It was not like the screaming of Fa when she was bearing the baby that died, or the mourning of Nil when Mal was buried; it was like the noise the horse makes when the cat sinks its curved teeth into the neck and hangs there, sucking blood. Lok was screaming himself without knowing it and fighting with thorns. And his senses told him through the screaming that Liku was doing what no man and no woman could do. She was moving away across the river.

Lok was still fighting with bushes when the screaming stopped. Now he could hear the laugh-noise again and the new one mewing. He burst the bushes and was out in the open by the dead tree. The clearing round the trunk stank of other and Liku and fear. Across the water there was a great bowing and ducking and swishing of green sprays. He caught a glimpse of Liku's red head and the new one on a dark, hairy shoulder. He jumped up and down and shouted.

"Liku! Liku!"

The green drifts twitched together and the people on the island disappeared. Lok ran up and down along the river-bank under the dead tree with its nest of ivy. He was so close to the water that he thrust chunks of earth out that went splash into the current.

"Liku! Liku!"

The bushes twitched again. Lok steadied by the tree and gazed. A head and a chest faced him, half-hidden. There were white bone things behind the leaves and hair. The man had white bone things above his eyes and under the mouth so that his face was longer than a face should be. The man turned sideways in the bushes and looked at Lok along his shoulder. A stick rose upright and there was a lump of bone in the middle. Lok peered at the stick and the lump of bone and the small eyes in the bone things over the face. Suddenly Lok understood that the man was holding the stick out to him but neither he nor Lok could reach across the river. He would have laughed if it were not for the echo of the screaming in his head. The stick began to grow shorter at both ends. Then it shot out to full length again.

The dead tree by Lok's ear acquired a voice.

"Clop!"

His ears twitched and he turned to the tree. By his face there had grown a twig: a twig that smelt of other, and of goose, and of the bitter berries that Lok's stomach told him he must not eat. This twig had a white bone at the end. There were hooks in the bone and sticky brown stuff hung in the crooks. His nose examined this stuff and did not like it. He smelled along the shaft of the twig. The leaves on the twig were red feathers and reminded him of goose. He was lost in a generalized astonishment and excitement. He shouted at the green drifts across the glittering water and heared Liku crying out in answer but

96

could not catch the words, They were cut off suddenly as though someone had clapped a hand over her mouth. He rushed to the edge of the water and came back. On either side of the open bank the bushes grew thickly in the flood; they waded out until at their farthest some of the leaves were opening under water; and these bushes leaned over.

The echo of Liku's voice in his head sent him trembling at this perilous way of bushes towards the island. He dashed at them where normally they would have been rooted on dry land and his feet splashed. He threw himself forward and grabbed at the branches with hands and feet. He shouted:

"I am coming!"

Half-lying, half-crawling, grinning all the time with fear he moved out over the river. He could see the wetness down there, mysterious and pierced everywhere by the dark and bending stems. There was no place that would support his whole weight. He had to spread it not only through all his limbs and body but be always in two places, moving, moving as the boughs gave. The water under him darkened. There were ripples on the surface behind each bough, weed caught and fluttering lengthwise, random flashes of the sun below and above. He came to the last tall bushes that were half-drowned and hung over the bed of the river itself. For a moment he saw a stretch of water and the island. He glimpsed the pillars of spray by the fall, saw the rocks of the cliff. Then, because he no longer moved, the branches began to bend under him. They swayed outwards and down so that his head was lower than his feet. He sank, gibbering, and the water rose, bringing a Lok-face with it. There was a

97

tremble of light over the Lok-face but he could see the teeth. Below the teeth, a weed-tail was moving backwards and forwards, more than the length of a man each time. But everything else under the teeth and the ripple was remote and dark. A breeze blew along the river and the bushes swayed gently sideways. His hands and feet gripped painfully of themselves and every muscle of his body was knotted. He ceased to think of the old people or the new people. He experienced Lok, upside down over deep water with a twig to save him.

Lok had never been so near the middle of water before. There was a skin on it and under the skin specks of dark stuff rose towards the surface, turned over and over, floated in circles or sank away out of sight. There were stones down there that glimmered greenly and wavered in the water Regularly the weed-tail eclipsed and revealed them. The breeze died away; the bushes bowed and lifted rhythmically as the weed-tail, so that the shining skin moved to and from his face. Pictures had gone from his head. Even fear was a dullness like the ache of hunger. Each hand and foot clung implacably to a sheaf of branches and the teeth grinned in the water.

The weed-tail was shortening. The green tip was withdrawing up river. There was a darkness that was consuming the other end. The darkness became a thing of complex shape, of sluggish and dreamlike movement. Like the specks of dirt, it turned over but not aimlessly. It was touching near the root of the weed-tail, bending the tail, turning over, rolling up the tail towards him. The arms moved a little and the eyes shone as dully as the stones. They revolved with the body, gazing at the surface, at the width of deep water and the hidden bottom with no trace of life or speculation. A skein of weed drew across the face and the eyes did not blink. The body turned with the same smooth and heavy motion as the river itself until its back was towards him rising along the weed-tail. The head turned towards him with dreamlike slowness, rose in the water, came towards his face.

Lok had always been awed by the old woman though she was his mother. She lived too near the great Oa in heart and head for a man to look upon her without dread. She knew so much, she had lived so long, she felt things they could only guess at, she was the woman. Though she wrapped them all in her understanding and compassion there was sometimes a remote stillness in what she did that left them humble and abashed. Therefore they loved her and dreaded her without fear, and they dropped their eyes before her. But now Lok saw her face to face and eye to eye, close. She was ignoring the injuries to her body, her mouth was open, the tongue showing and the specks of dirt were circling slowly in and out as though it had been nothing but a hole in a stone. Her eyes swept across the bushes, across his face, looked through him without seeing him, rolled away and were gone.

SIX

Lok's feet unclenched themselves from the bushes. They slid down and he was hanging by his arms and up to the waist in water. He raised his knees and his hair pricked. He was past screaming. The terror of the water was only a background. He flung himself round, grabbed more branches and floundered through the bushes and the water to the bank. He stood there, his back to the river, and shivered like Mal. His teeth were showing and he had his arms raised and tensed as though he were still holding himself above the water. He was looking slightly up and his head was turning from side to side. Behind him the laugh-noises began again. Little by little they took his attention though the posture and grin of strain stayed in his body. There were many laugh-noises as though the new people had gone mad and there was one louder than the rest, a man's voice, shouting. The other voices ceased and the man went on shouting. A woman laughed, shrill and excited. Then there was silence.

The sun was making a stipple of bright spots over the undergrowth and the wet brown ground. At intervals a breeze would wander up river, making the new and vivid foliage turn slightly to a new direction so that the spots were sifted and resprinkled. A fox barked sharply among the rocks. A pair of woodpigeons spoke to each other of nesting time monotonously.

Slowly his head and arms came down. He no longer grinned. He took a step forward and turned. Then he began to run down river, not fast, but keeping as near to the water as he could. He peered seriously into the bushes, walked, stopped. His eyes unfocused and the grin came back. He stood, his hand resting on the curved bough of a beech and looked at nothing. He examined the bough, holding it with both hands. He began to sway it, backwards and forwards, backwards and forwards, faster and faster. The great fan of branches on the end went swishing over the tops of the bushes, Lok hurled himself backwards and forwards, he was gasping and the sweat of his body was running down his legs with the water of the river. He let go, sobbing, and stood again, arms bent, head tilted, his teeth clenched as if every nerve in his body were burning. The woodpigeons went on talking and the spots of sunlight sifted over him.

He moved from the beech, back along the trail, faltered, stopped, then began to run. He flashed into the open space where the dead tree was and the sun was bright on the tuft of red feathers. He looked towards the island, saw the bushes move, then one of the twigs came twirling across the river and vanished beyond him in the forest. He had a confused idea that someone was trying to give him a present. He would have smiled across at the bone-faced man but no one was visible there and the open space was still full of the faint excruciating echo of Liku screaming. He wrenched the twig from the tree and started to run again. He came to the slope up to the mountain and the terrace and checked at the scent of other and Liku; and then he was following the scent back through time towards the overhang. He moved so fast, pressing down with the knuckles, that were it not for the arrow he held in his left hand he would have seemed to be running on all fours. He put the twig crosswise in his mouth between his teeth, reached out with both hands, half-ran, half-clambered up the slope. When he was near the entry to the terrace he could see over the rock down to the island. One of the bone-faced men was visible there from the chest up, the rest of him hidden by bushes. The new people had never shown up at such a distance before in daylight, and now the face looked like the white patch on a deer's rump. There was smoke behind the new man among the trees, but blue and transparent. The pictures in Lok's head were very confused and too many —worse than no pictures at all. He took the twig from his teeth. He did not know what he shouted.

"I am coming with Fa!"

He ran through the entry and was on the terrace, and no one was about, he saw that, felt it as a coldness coming from the overhang where the fire had been. He went quickly up the earthen rise and stood looking in. The fire had been thrown about and the only one of the people left was Mal under his hump. But there were smells and signs in plenty. He heard a noise on the top of the overhang, leapt out of the circle of ashes and there was Fa coming down the ledges of rock. She saw him and they flew together. She was shuddering and she held him tightly with both her arms. They babbled at each other.

"The bone-face men gave it me. I ran up the slope. Liku screamed across the water."

"When you went down the rock. I am climbing the rocks because I am frightened. Men came to the overhang."

They were silent, clinging and shuddering. The pack of unsorted pictures that flickered between them tired them both. They looked in each other's eyes helplessly and then Lok began to turn his head restlessly from side to side.

"The fire is dead."

They went to the fire, holding each other. Fa squatted and poked about among the charred ends of branches. The hand of habit was on them. They squatted each in the appropriate place and looked out dumbly at the water and the silver line where it poured over the cliff. There was evening sun slanting into the overhang now but no ruddy, flickering light for it to contend with. Fa stirred and spoke at last.

"Here is the picture. I am looking down. The men come and I hide. As I hide I see the old woman go to meet them."

"She was in the water. She looked at me out of the water. I was upside down."

Again they gazed at each other helplessly.

"I come down to the terrace when the men go away. They have Liku and the new one."

The air round Lok echoed with the phantom screaming.

"Liku screamed across the river. She is on the island."

"I do not see this picture."

Neither did Lok. He spread his arms wide and grinned at the memory of the screaming.

"This twig came to me from the island."

Fa examined the twig closely from the barbed bone-point to the red feathers and the smooth nock at the end. She returned to the barbs and wrinkled up her face at the brown gum. Lok's pictures were a little better sorted.

"Liku is on the island with the other people."

"The new people."

"They threw this twig across the river into the dead tree."

"?"

Lok tried to make her see a picture with him but his head was too tired and he gave up.

"Come!"

They followed the scent from the blood to the edge of the river. There was blood on the rock by the water too and a little milk. Fa pressed her hands on her head and gave her picture words.

"They killed Nil and threw her into the water. And the old woman."

"They have taken Liku and the new one."

Now they shared a picture that was a purpose. They ran together along the terrace. At the corner Fa held back but when Lok climbed round she followed him and they stood on the rock-face looking down at the island. They could see the faint blue smoke still spreading in the evening light; but very soon there would be the shadow of the mountains on the forest. Pictures fitted together in Lok's head. He saw himself turning out on the cliff to speak to the old woman because he had smelt fire when she was not there. But this was only another complication in a day of total newness and he let the picture be. The bushes were shaking on the shore of the island. Fa seized Lok by the wrist and they shrank down against the rock. The shaking was prolonged and excited.

Then the two people became nothing but eyes that looked and absorbed and were without thought. There was a log under the bushes floating in the water and one end of it was swinging out into the stream. It was dark and smooth, and hollow. One of the bone-face men sat in it at the end that was swinging out. The branches that hid the other end dragged on a sort of lump; and there it was, free of the bushes, floating, and a man at either end. The log pointed up towards the fall and a little across the river. The current was beginning to take it back downstream. The two men lifted sticks that ended in great brown leaves which they stuck into the water. The log steadied, remained in the same place with the river moving under it. Patches of white foam and swirling green were tailing away down river from the brown leaves. The log sidled out and there was a stretch of uncrossable deep water on either side. The people could see how the men peered at the bank by the dead tree and into the undergrowth on either side through the little holes in their masks of bone.

The man in the front of the log put his stick down and took up a bent one instead. There was a bunch of red feathers by his waist. He held this stick by the middle as he had done when the twig flew across the river to Lok. The log sidled into the bank and the man in the front jumped forward so that he was hidden by the bushes. The log stayed where it was and the man in the back end dug his brown leaf into the water every now and then. The shadow from the fall was reaching him. They could see how the hair grew on his head above the bone. It made a massive clump like a rook's nest in a tall tree and every time he tugged at the leaf, it bobbed and quivered.

Fa was quivering too.

"Will he come to the terrace?"

But then the first man appeared. The

nosed out of sight against the bank and when it reappeared the first man was sitting again, and he held
another twig in his hand with red feathers at the end.
The log turned out towards the fall, both men were
dipping their leaves together. The log sidled out into
deep water.

Lok began to babble.

"Liku crossed the river in the log. Where does such a
log grow? Now Liku will come back in the log and we
shall be together."

He pointed down to the men in the log.

"They have twigs."

The log was returning to the island. It was nosing at
the bushes by the shore like a water-rat examining something to eat. The man in the front end stood up carefully.
He parted the bushes and hauled himself and the log
through. The other end swung slowly downstream, then
drew forward until the hanging branches covered it so
that the man at the back ducked and laid down his
stick.

Suddenly Fa seized Lok by his right arm and shook
him. She was staring into his face.

"Give the twig back!"

He shared some of the fright in her face. Behind her
the sun made a slope of shadow stretch from the lip of
the fall to the end of the island. Beyond her right
shoulder he glimpsed a trunk of wood, upending and
disappearing without noise over the fall. He lifted the
twig and examined it.

"Throw it. Now."

He jerked his head violently.

"No! No! The new people threw it to me."

Fa took two steps back and forth on the rock. She looked quickly towards the cold overhang, then at the island. She took him by both shoulders and shook him.

"The new people have many pictures. And I have many pictures too."

Lok laughed, uncertainly.

"A man for pictures. A woman for Oa."

Her fingers tightened on his flesh. Her face looked as though she hated him.

She spoke fiercely:

"What will the new one do without Nil's milk? Who will find food for Liku?"

He scratched in the hair under his open mouth. She took her hands away and waited for a moment. Lok continued to scratch and there was an aching emptiness in his head. She jerked twice.

"Lok has no pictures in his head."

She became very solemn and there was the great Oa, not seen but sensed like a cloud round her. Lok felt himself diminish. He clasped his twig with both hands nervously and looked away. Now that the forest was dark he could see the eye of the new peoples' fire blinking at him. Fa spoke to the side of his head.

"Do what I say. Do not say: 'Fa do this.' I will say: 'Lok do this.' I have many pictures."

He diminished a little more, glanced quickly at her, then at the distant fire.

"Throw the twig."

He swung back his right arm and hurled the twig feathers foremost into the air. The feathers dragged, the shaft swung round, the twig hung for a moment in the sunlight, then the point dropped and the whole twig entered the shadows as smoothly as a stooping hawk, slid down and vanished in the water.

He heard Fa make a choking sound, a kind of dry sob: then she was holding him and her head was against his neck and she was laughing and sobbing and shaking as though she had done something difficult but good. She became Fa without much Oa and he put his arms round her for comfort. The sun was right down in the gap and the river flamed so that the edge of the fall was burning bright as the ends of sticks in the fire. There were dark logs coming down river, black against the flaming water. There were whole trees, their roots behaving like strange creatures of the sea. One was turning towards the fall beneath them; roots and branches lifting, dragging, going down. It hung for a moment on the lip; the burning water made a great heap of light over the end and then the tree was going down the air to vanish as smoothly as the twig.

Lok spoke over Fa's shoulder.

"The old woman was in the water."

Presently Fa pushed him away from her.

"Come!"

He followed her round the corner into the level light of the terrace and their bodies wove a parallel skein of shadows as they walked so that a lifted arm seemed to lift a long weight of darkness with it. They went by habit up the rise to the overhang but it was empty of comfort. The recesses were there, dark eyes, and between them the pillar rock, lit redly. The sticks and ashes were so much earth. Fa sat on the ground by the hearth and frowned at the island. Lok waited while she pressed her hands on her head but he could not share her pictures. He remembered the meat in the recesses.

"Food."

Fa said nothing, so Lok, a little timidly, as if he might still have to meet the old woman's eye, felt his way into a recess. He smelled at the meat and brought enough for both of them. When he returned he heard the hyenas yelping on the rocks above the overhang. Fa took meat without seeing Lok and began to eat, still looking at her pictures.

Once he had begun to eat, Lok was reminded of his hunger. He tore the muscle in long strips from the bone and stuffed it in his mouth. There was much strength in the meat.

Fa spoke indistinctly.

"We throw stones at the yellow ones."

"?"

"The twig."

They ate again in silence as the hyenas whined and yelped. Lok's ears told him they were hungry and his nose assured him that they were alone. He picked in the bone for marrow, then took up an unburnt stick from by the dead fire and thrust it in as far as he could. He had a sudden picture of Lok thrusting a stick into a crack for honey. A feeling rushed into him like a wave of the sea, swallowing his contentment in the food, swallowing even the companionship of Fa. He crouched there, the stick still in the hollow bone, and the feeling went through him and over him. It came from nowhere like the river, and like the river it would not be denied. Lok was a log in the river, a drowned animal that the waters treat as they will. He raised his head as Nil had raised her head and the sound of mourning broke from him while the sunlight lifted from the gap and the dusk came welling through. Then he was close to Fa and she was holding him.

The moon had risen when they moved. Fa stood up and squinted at it then looked at the island. She went down to the river and drank and stayed there, kneeling. Lok stood by her.

"Fa."

She made a motion with her hand of not to be disturbed and went on looking at the water. Then she was up and running along the terrace.

"The log! The log!"

Lok ran after her but could not understand. She was pointing at a slim trunk that was sliding towards them and turning as it went. She threw herself on her knees and grabbed a long splinter from the bigger end. The log turned and pulled at her. Lok saw her slip on the rock and dived at her feet. He got her round the knee; and then they were straining landward and the other end of the log was circling round. Fa had one hand wound in his hair and was pulling it without mercy so that the water stood in his eyes, swelled and ran down to his mouth. The other end of the log swung in, and it was floating by the terrace, pulling at them only gently. Fa spoke over her back.

"I have a picture of us crossing to the island on the log."

Lok's hair bristled.

"But men cannot go over the fall like a log!"

"Be silent!"

She puffed for a while and got her breath back.

"Up at the other end of the terrace we can rest the log across to the rock." She blew her breath out hugely.

"The people cross the water on the trail by running along a log."

Then Lok was frightened.

"We cannot go over the fall!"

Fa explained again, patiently.

They towed the log upstream to the end of the terrace. This was a difficult and hair-bristling job because the terrace was not at an even height above the water and there were gaps and outcrops along the edge of it. They had to learn as they went: and all the time the water tugged, now gently, now with sudden strength as though they were robbing it of food. The log was not as dead as firewood. Sometimes it twisted in their hands and the broken branches of the slenderer end would twitch over the rock like legs. Long before they had reached the end of the terrace Lok had forgotten why they were towing it. He only remembered the sudden enlargement of Fa and the wave of misery that had drowned him. Working at the log, frightened of the water, the misery receded to a point where it could be examined and he did not like it. The misery was connected with the people and with strangeness.

"Liku will be hungry."

Fa said nothing.

By the time they had worked the log to the end of the terrace the moon was their only light. The gap was blue and white, and the flat river laced all over with silver.

"Hold the end."

While he held it, Fa pushed the other end away from

her into the river but the current brought it back. Then she squatted for a long time with her hands over her head and Lok waited in obedient dumbness. He yawned widely, licked his lips and looked at the sheer blue cliff on the other side of the gap. There was no terrace on that side of the river but only a sharp drop into deep water. He yawned again and put up both hands to wipe the tears out of his eyes. He blinked awhile at the night, inspected the moon, and scratched himself under his lip.

Fa cried out:

"The log!"

He peered down past his feet but the log had gone; he looked this way and that and flinchingly into the air; then he saw it drifting by Fa and turning away slightly. She scrambled along the rock and grabbed at the leg-like branches. The trunk dragged her, checked, then the end that Lok had forgotten began to swing outward. He made motions of catching hold but the log was out of reach. Fa was chattering and screaming at him in rage. He backed away from her sheepishly. He was saying "The log, the log——" to himself without meaning. The misery had withdrawn like the tide but it was there still.

The other end of the log thumped against the tail of the island. The water of the river pushed sideways against it and the log turned, grinding, pulling the branch out of Fa's hand. The branch scarred down the terrace, bent, flicked, bent again and gave with a long crackle. The log was jammed, the thicker end bumped on the rock, bump, bump, bump; the water made a sluice over the middle, and the crown was crushed in the uneven side of the terrace. The middle of the log, though it was nearly as thick as Lok, bent under the pressure of the water for it was many times as long as a man.

Fa came close to him and looked doubtfully in his face. Lok remembered her anger when the log had seemed to go away from them. He patted her shoulder anxiously.

"I have many pictures."

She looked silently. Then she grinned and patted him back. She put both hands on her thighs and beat them softly, laughing at him so that he patted and laughed with her. The moon was so bright now that two grey-blue shadows imitated them at their feet.

A hyena whined by the overhang. Lok and Fa scuttered over the terrace toward them. Without a word their pictures were one picture. By the time they were near enough to see the hyenas each had stones in either hand and they were wide apart. They began to snarl and yell together and then the prick-eared shapes had fled up the rock to slink and sidle there, grey, with four eyes like green sparks.

Fa took the rest of the food from the recess and the hyenas snarled after them as they ran back along the terrace. By the time they reached the log they were eating mechanically. Then Lok took the bone from his lips.

"It is for Liku."

The log was not alone. Another smaller one lay alongside it, bumping and grinding and the water flowed over both. Fa went forward in the moonlight and laid a foot on the shoreward end. Then she came back and grimaced at the water. She walked away up the terrace, glanced downstream to where the lip of the fall was flickering and then raced forward. She baulked, checked, stopped. A large stick, turning in the water, added itself to the two logs. She tried again with a shorter run and stopped to gibber at the dazzling water. She began to run round by the logs, not speaking proper words but sounding fierce and desperate. This was another new thing and it frightened Lok so that he edged away over the terrace. But then he remembered his own antics by the log in the forest and made himself laugh at her, though there was an emptiness on her back. She ran at him and her teeth grinned in his face as though she would bite him and strange sounds were coming out of her mouth. His body jumped back.

She was silent, clinging to him and trembling, they were one shadow on the rock. She muttered to him in a voice that had no Oa in it:

"Go first on the log."

Lok put her to one side. Now they made no noise the misery was back. He looked at the log, found there was outside of Lok and inside and that outside was better. He hung the meat for Liku firmly from his teeth. She was not riding him and with Fa trembling and the river moving sideways, he did not care to be funny. He inspected the log from end to end, noted a broad bit on this side of the sluice where there had once been the division of a limb and walked away up the terrace. He measured the distance, leaned and rushed forward. The log was under his foot and slippery. It was trembling like Fa, it was moving sideways up the river so that he swayed to the right to retrieve himself. Unaccountably he was falling. His foot came down full force on the other log which sank and he stumbled. His left leg thrust, he was up and the sluice was pushing with more force than a great wind at the crooks of his knees and cold as ice women. He

leapt frantically, stumbled, leapt and then he was claw-
ing at the rock, reaching up, holding the top of it with his
face pressed in Liku's meat. His feet walked away from
each other up the rock until he felt that his crutch would
split. He hitched himself painfully round the rock and
faced back at Fa. He found that a sound had been coming
out of his mouth for all the meat, high and sustained as
Nil's sound when she ran on the log in the forest. He fell
silent, breathing jerkily. There was another log adding
itself to the pile. It lay alongside, bumping, and the sluice
broke into foam and sparkling places. Fa tried this log
with her feet. She walked carefully along over the water,
straddling, with a foot on each log. She reached the rock
where he lay and climbed up beside him. She shouted to
him over the noise of the water:

"I did not make a noise."

Lok straightened up and tried to pretend that the rock
was not moving with them up river. Fa gauged the leap
and landed neatly on the next one. He followed her,
empty-headed for the noise and newness. They jumped
and clambered until they came to a rock that had bushes
at the top, and when they reached this Fa lay down and
gripped her fingers in the earth while Lok waited
patiently with his hands full of meat. They were on the
island, and on either side of them the lip of the fall ran
and flickered like summer lightning. There was also a
new noise, the voice of the main fall beyond the island
which was nearer to them than ever before. There was no
competing with it. Even the sketch of sound that the
smaller fall left of their voices was taken clean away.

Presently Fa sat up. She went forward until she was
looking down the shin of the island and Lok went to her.

The foot spread and by the ankle the drifts of water smoke ate inward so that they left only a narrowing way down. Lok crouched and looked over.

Ivy and roots, scars of earth and knobs of jagged rock —the cliff leaned over so that the top with its plume of birch was looking straight down on to the island. The rocks that had fallen were still jumbled against the cliff at the bottom and their dark shapes, always wet, contrasted with the grey gleam of the leaves and the cliff. Trees still lived at the top, though perilously after the rock had torn most of their roots away. What remained were clutched into the crevices in the lip or writhed down the cliff or ended pointlessly in the wet air. The water poured out and down on either side, foamed and flashed, and the solid earth quivered. The moon, nearly full, fronted the cliff high up and the fire glowed in the farthest reach of the island.

The people made no comment on the dizzy height. They leaned out and searched the face of the cliff for a pathway. Fa slid over the edge, her blue shadow more visible than her body, and let herself hand over foot down the roots and the ivy. Lok followed, the meat in his teeth once more, squinting when he could at the glow of the fire. He felt a great impulse to hurry towards it as though there were some remedy by it for his misery. Nor was this remedy only Liku and the new one. The other people with their many pictures were like water that at once horrifies and at the same time dares and invites a man to go near it. He was obscurely aware of this attraction without definition and it made him foolish. He found himself at the end of a huge broken root in a wilderness of glittering, cavernous water. The root was swinging with his weight so that the meat flopped on his chest. He had to jump sideways to the tangle of roots and ivy before he could follow Fa again.

She led the way over the rocks and into the forest of the island. There was little here that might be called a trail. The other people had left their scent among smashed bushes and that was all. Fa followed the scent without reason. She knew the fire must be at the other end but to say why, she would have had to stop and wrestle with pictures, holding her hands to her head. There were many birds nesting on the island and they resented the people so that Fa and Lok began to move with great care. They ceased to pay direct attention to the new scent and adjusted themselves to threading the forest with as little noise and disturbance as possible. Their pictures were shared busily. In the almost total darkness under the coverts they saw with night sight; they avoided the invisible, lifted aside the clinging ivy, undid the draped brambles and sidled through. Soon they could hear the new people.

They could see the fire too; or rather they could see the reflection of the fire and a flicker. The light made the rest of the island impenetrable dark and clouded their night sight so that they were slower. The fire was much bigger than before and the lighted patch was surrounded with a fringe of new leaves that were pale green as though there was some sort of sunlight behind them. The people were making a rhythmic noise like the beat of a heart. Fa stood up in front of Lok so that she became a densely black shape.

The trees were tall at this end of the island and in the centre the bushes were spaced so that there was room to move among them. Lok followed her until they were standing with bent knees and toes flexed for flight behind one of the bushes at the very edge of the firelight. They could just see over into the patch of open ground that the people had chosen. There were too many things to see at once. To begin with, the trees had reorganized themselves. They had crouched down and woven their branches closely so that they made caverns of darkness on either side of the fire. The new people sat on the ground between Lok and the light and no two heads were the same shape. They were pulled out sideways into horns, or spired like a pine tree or were round and huge. Beyond the fire he could see the ends of the pile of logs that was waiting to be burnt and for all their weight the light seemed to make them move.

Then, incredibly, a rutting stag belled by the trunks. The noise was harsh and furious, full of pain and desire. It was the voice of the greatest of all stags and the world was not wide enough for him. Fa and Lok gripped each other and stared at the logs without a picture. The new people bent so that their shapes changed and the heads were hidden. The stag appeared. He moved springily on his two hind legs and his forelegs were stretched out sideways. His antlered head was among the leaves of the trees, he was looking up, past the new people, past Fa and Lok, and it swayed from side to side. The stag began to turn and they saw that his tail was dead and flapped against the pale, hairless legs. He had hands.

In one of the caverns they heard the new one mew. Lok jumped up and down behind the bush.

"Liku!"

Fa had him by the mouth and was holding him still.

The stag stopped dancing. They heard Liku calling.

"Here I am, Lok. Here I am!"

There was a sudden clamour of the laugh-noise, dive and twist and scribble of bird-noise, all voices, shouting, a woman screaming. The fire gave a sudden hiss and white steam shot out of it while the light dulled. The new people were flitting to and fro. There was anger and fear.

"Liku!"

The stag was swaying violently in the dim light. Fa was tugging at Lok and muttering at him. The people were coming with sticks, bent and straight.

"Quickly!"

A man was beating savagely at the bush to the right. Lok swung back his arm.

"The food is for Liku!"

He hurled it into the clearing. The lump fell by the stag's feet. Lok had just time to see the stag bend towards it in the steam and then he was stumbling while Fa pulled him. The clamour of the new people was sinking into a purposeful series of shouts, questions and answers, orders—burning branches were racing through the clearing, so that fans of spring foliage leapt into being and disappeared. Lok put down his head and thrust against the soft earth with his feet. There was a hiss as of suddenly indrawn breath close over his head. Fa and Lok swerved among the bushes and slowed. They began to perform their miracle of sensitive ingenuity with the brambles and branches; but this time Lok caught desperation from Fa and her hard breathing. They hurled themselves along and the torches flared under the trees behind them. They heard the new people calling to each other and making a great noise in the undergrowth. Then a single voice cried out loudly. The crashing stopped.

Fa scrabbled at the wet rocks.

"Quickly! Quickly!"

He could just hear her for all the thunder of the glittering skeins of water. Obediently he followed her, astonished at her speed, but with no picture in his head unless it was the meaningless one of the stag dancing.

Fa threw herself over the lip of the cliff and lay down on her shadow. Lok waited. She gasped at him.

"Where are they?"

Lok peered down at the island but she interrupted him.

"Are they climbing?"

Half-way down the cliff a root was swaying slowly from the tug that she had given it but the rest of the cliff was motionless, looking at the moon.

"No!"

They were silent for a time. Lok noticed the noise of the water again and as he did so the noise became something so loud that he could not speak through it. He wondered idly whether they had shared pictures or spoken with their mouths and then he examined the feeling of heaviness in his head and body. There was no doubt at all. The feeling was connected with Liku. He yawned, wiped his eye-hollows with his fingers and licked his lips. Fa got to her feet.

"Come!"

They trotted between the birches over the island, jumped from stone to stone. The log had gathered others so that they lay close together, more than the fingers of a hand they were, and tangled with all the drifting stuff of this side of the river. The water was spurting between them and flowering over. It was as broad a trail as the one through the forest. They reached the terrace easily and stood without speech.

There was a scuffling noise coming from the overhang. They ran quickly and the grey hyenas fled away. The moon shone clear into the overhang so that even the recesses were lighted and the only dark thing was the hole where Mal had been buried. They knelt and swept back the dirt, the ashes and bones over the part of his body they could see. Now the earth did not rise in a hump but was level with the topmost hearth again. Still without speech they rolled a stone and made Mal safe.

Fa muttered.

"How will they feed the new one without milk?"

Then they were holding on to each other, breast against breast. The rocks round them were like any other rocks; the firelight had died out of them. The two pressed themselves against each other, they clung, searching for a centre, they fell, still clinging face to face. The fire of their bodies lit, and they strained towards it.

SEVEN

Fa pushed him to one side. They stood up together and looked round the overhang. The bleak air of first dawn poured round them. Fa went into a recess and came back with an almost meatless bone and some scraps that the hyenas had not been able to reach. The people were red again, copper red and sandy for the blue and grey of the night had left them. They said nothing but picked away and shared the scraps with a passion of pity for each other. Presently they wiped their hands on their thighs and went down to the water and drank. Then still without speaking or sharing a picture they turned to the left and went to the corner round which lay the cliff.

Fa stopped.

"I do not want to see."

Together they turned and looked at the empty overhang.

"I will take fire when it falls from the sky or wakes among the heather."

Lok considered the picture of fire. Otherwise there was an emptiness in his head and only the tidal feeling, deep and sure, was noticeable inside him. He began to walk towards the logs at the other end of the terrace. Fa caught him by the wrist.

"We shall not go again on the island."

Lok faced her, his hands up.

"There must be food found for Liku. So that she will be strong when she comes back."

Fa looked deeply at him and there were things in her face that he could not understand. He took a step sideways shrugged, gesticulated. He stopped and waited anxiously.

"No!"

She held him by the wrist and lugged him. He resisted, talking all the time. He did not know what he said. She stopped pulling and faced him again.

"You will be killed."

There was a pause. Lok looked at her, then at the island. He scratched his left cheek. Fa came close.

"I shall have children that do not die in the cave by the sea. There will be a fire."

"Liku will have children when she is a woman."

She let go of his wrist again.

"Listen. Do not speak. The new people took the log and Mal died. Ha was on the cliff and a new man was on the cliff. Ha died. The new people came to the overhang. Nil and the old woman died."

The light was much stronger behind her. There was a fleck of red in the sky over her head. She grew in his sight. She was the woman. Lok shook his head at her, humbly. Her words had made the feeling rise.

"When the new people bring Liku back I shall be glad."

Fa made a high, angry sound, she took a step to the water and came back again. She grabbed him by his shoulders.

"How can they give the new one milk? Does a stag give milk? And what if they do not bring back Liku?"

He answered humbly out of an empty head.

"I do not see this picture."

She left him in her anger, turned away and stood with a hand on the corner where the cliff began. He could see how she was bristling and how the muscles of her shoulder twitched. She was bent, leaning forward, right hand on right knee. He heard her mutter at him with her back still turned.

"You have fewer pictures than the new one."

Lok put the heels of his hands in his eyes and pressed so that spokes of light flashed in them like the river.

"There has not been a night."

That was real. Where the night should have been was a greyness. Not only his ears and his nose had been awake after they had lain together, but the Lok inside them, watching the feeling rise and ebb and rise. There was stuffed inside the bones of his head the white flock of the autumn creepers, their seeds were in his nose, making him yawn and sneeze. He put his hands apart and blinked at where Fa had been. Now she was backed on this side of the rock and peering round it at the river. Her hand beckoned.

The log was out again. It was near the island and the same two bone faces were sitting at either end. They were digging the water and the log was sidling across the river. When it was near the bank and the swarming bushes it straightened into the current and the men stopped digging. They were looking closely at the clear patch by the water where the dead tree was. Lok could see how one turned and spoke to the other.

Fa touched his hand.

"They are looking for something."

The log drifted gently downstream with the current and the sun was rising. The farther reaches of the river burst into flame, so that for a time the forest on either side was dark by contrast. The indefinable attraction of the new people pushed the flock out of Lok's head. He forgot to blink.

The log was smaller, drifting down away from the fall. When it turned askew, the man in the back would dig again and the log would point straight at Lok's eyes. Always, the two men looked sideways at the bank.

Fa muttered:

"There is another log."

The bushes by the island shore were shaking busily. They parted for a moment and now that he knew where to look Lok could see the end of another log hidden close in. A man thrust his head and shoulders through the green leaves and waved an arm angrily. The two men in the log began to dig quickly until it had moved right up to where the man waved opposite the dead tree. Now they were no longer looking at the dead tree but at the man, and nodding their heads at him. The log brought them to him and nosed under the bushes.

Curiosity overcame Lok; he began to run towards the new way on to the island so excitedly that Fa shared his picture. She got him again, and grabbed him.

"No! No!"

Lok jabbered. Fa shouted at him.

"I say 'No!'"

She pointed at the overhang.

"What did you say? Fa has many pictures——"

At last he was silent and waiting for her. She spoke solemnly.

"We shall go down into the forest. For food. We shall watch them across the river."

They ran down the slope away from the river, keeping the rocks between them and the new people. In the skirts of the forest there was food; bulbs that just showed a point of green, grubs and shoots, fungi, the tender inside of some kinds of bark. The meat of the doe was still in them and they were not hungry as the people counted hunger. They could eat, where there was food; but without it they could go for to-day easily and for to-morrow if they had to. For this reason there was no urgency in their searching so that presently the enchantment of the new people drew them again to the bushes at the edge of the water. They stood, toes gripped in the mire, and listened for the new people through the noise of the fall. An early fly buzzed at Lok's nose. The air was warm and the sun softly bright so that he yawned again. Then he heard the new people making their bird-noises of conversation and a number of other unexplained sounds, bumps and creakings. Fa sneaked to the edge of the clearing by the dead tree and lay on the earth.

There was nothing to be seen across the water, yet the bumps and creaks continued.

"Fa. Climb the dead trunk, to see."

She turned her face and looked at him doubtfully. All at once he realized that she was going to say no, was going to insist that they went away from the new people and put a great gap of time between them and Liku; and this became a knowledge that was unbearable. He sneaked quickly forward on all fours and ran up the concealed side of the dead tree. In a moment he was burrowing through the shock-head among the dusty, dark, sour-smelling ivy leaves. He had hardly lifted his last limb into the hollow top before Fa's head broke through behind him.

The top of the tree was empty like a great acorn cup. It was white, soft wood that gave and moulded to their weight and was full of food. The ivy spread upwards and downwards in a dark tangle so that they might have been sitting in a bush on the ground. The other trees over-topped them but there was open sky towards the river and the green drifts of the island. Parting the leaves cautiously as if he were looking for eggs, Lok found that he could make a hole no bigger than the eye-part of his face; and though the edges of the hole moved a little he could see the river and the other banks, all the brighter for the dark green leaves round the hole—as though he had cupped his hands and was looking through them. On his left Fa was making herself a lookout, and the edge of the cup even gave her something to rest her elbows on. The heavy feeling sank in Lok as it always did when he had the new people to watch. He sagged luxuriously. Then suddenly they forgot everything else and were very still.

The log was sliding out of the bushes by the island. The two men were digging carefully and the log was turning. It did not point at Lok and Fa but upstream, though it began to move across river towards them. There were many new things in the hollow of the log; shapes like rocks and bulging skins. There were all kinds of stick, from long poles without leaves or branches to sprays of withering green. The log came close.

At last they saw the new people face to face and in sun-light. They were incomprehensibly strange. Their hair was black and grew in the most unexpected ways. The bone-face in the front of the log had a pine-tree of hair that stood straight up so that his head, already too long, was drawn out as though something were pulling it upward without mercy. The other bone-face had hair in a huge bush that stood out on all sides like the ivy on the dead tree.

There was hair growing thickly over their bodies about the waist, the belly and the upper part of the leg so that this part of them was thicker than the rest. Yet Lok did not look immediately at their bodies; he was far too absorbed in the stuff round their eyes. A piece of white bone was placed under them, fitting close, and where the broad nostrils should have shown were narrow slits and between them the bone was drawn out to a point. Under that was another slit over the mouth, and their voices came fluttering through it. There was a little dark hair jutting out under the slit. The eyes of the face that peered through all this bone were dark and busy. There were eyebrows above them, thinner than the mouth or the nostrils, black, curving out and up so that the men looked menacing and wasp-like. Lines of teeth and sea-shells hung round their necks, over grey, furry skin. Over the eyebrows the bone bulged up and swept back to be hidden under the hair. As the log came closer, Lok could see that the colour was not really bone white and shining but duller. It was more the colour of the big fungi, the ears that the people ate, and something like them in texture. Their legs and arms were stick-thin so that the joints were like the nodes in a twig.

Now that Lok was looking almost into the log he saw that it was much broader than before; or rather that it was the two logs moving side by side. There were more bundles and curious shapes in this log and a man lay among them on his side. His body and bone was like the others but his hair grew on his head in a mass of sharp points that glistened and looked hard as the points on a chestnut case. He was doing something to one of the sharp twigs and his curved stick lay beside him.

The logs sidled right into the bank. The man at the back—Lok thought of him as Pine-tree—spoke softly. Bush laid down his wooden leaf and caught hold of the grass of the bank. Chestnut-head took his curved stick and twig and stole across the logs until he was crouched on the earth itself. Lok and Fa were almost directly above him. They could smell his individual scent, a sea-smell, meat-smell, fearsome and exciting. He was so close that any moment he might wind them for all he was below them and Lok inhibited his own scent in sudden fear, though he did not know what he did. He reduced his breathing till it was the merest surface and the very leaves were more lively.

Chestnut-head stood under them in the sun pattern. The twig was across the curved stick. He looked this way and that round the dead tree, he inspected the ground, he looked forward again into the forest. He spoke sideways to the others in the boat out of his slit; soft twittering speech; the whiteness quivered.

Lok felt the shock of a man who has trusted to a bough that is not there. He understood in a kind of upside-down sensation that there was no Mal face, Fa face, Lok face concealed under the bone. It was skin.

Bush and Pine-tree had done something with strips of hide that joined the logs to the bushes. They got quickly out of the log and ran forward out of sight. Presently there was the sound of someone striking stone against wood. Chestnut-head crept forward too and was hidden.

There was nothing of interest now but the logs. They were very smooth and shiny inside where the wood could be seen and outside there were long smears like the whiteness on a rock when the sea has gone back and the sun has dried it. The edges were rounded, depressed in places where the hands of the bone-faces had rested. The shapes inside them were too various and numerous to be sorted. There were round stones, sticks, hides, there were bundles bigger than Lok, there were patterns of vivid red, bones that had grown into live shapes, the very ends of the brown leaves where the men held them were shaped like brown fish, there were smells, there were questions and no answers. Lok looked without seeing and the picture slid apart and came together again. Across the water there was no movement on the island.

Fa touched him on the hand. She was turning herself in the tree. Lok followed her carefully and they made themselves spy-holes that looked down into the clearing.

Already the familiar had altered. The tangle of bush and stagnant water to the left of the clearing was the same and so was the impenetrable marsh to the right. But where the trail through the forest touched the clearing thorn bushes were now growing thickly. There was a gap in these bushes and as they watched they saw Pine-tree come through the gap with another thorn bush over his shoulder. The stem was clean white and pointed. In the forest behind him the noise of chopping went on.

Fear was coming from Fa. It was not a shared picture but a general sense, a bitter smell, a dead silence and agonized attention, a motionlessness and tensed awareness that began to call forth the same in him. Now, more clearly than ever before there were two Loks, outside and inside. The inner Lok could look for ever. But the outer that breathed and heard and smelt and was awake always, was insistent and tightening on him like another skin. It forced the knowledge of its fear, its sense of peril on him long before his brain could understand the picture. He was more frightened than ever before in his life, more than when he had crouched on a rock with Ha and a cat had paced to and fro by a drained kill, looking up and wondering whether they were worth the trouble.

Fa's mouth crept to his ear.

"We are shut in."

The thorn bushes spread. They were very thick where there was an easy way into the clearing; but there were others now, two lines of them by the stagnant water and by the marsh. The clearing was a half-ring open only to the water of the river. The three bone-faces came through the last gap, with more thorn bushes. With these they closed the way behind them.

Fa whispered in his ear.

"They know we are here. They do not want us to go away."

All the same the bone-faces ignored them. Bush and Pine-tree went back and the logs bumped each other. Chestnut-head began to pace slowly round the line of thorn bushes, keeping his face to the forest. Always the bent stick was held with a twig across it. The thorn bushes were up to his chest and when a bull bellowed far off on the plains he froze, face lifted and the stick unbent a little. The woodpigeons were talking again and the sun looked down into the top of the dead tree and breathed warmly on the two people.

Someone dug noisily in the water and the logs bumped. There were wooden knockings, draggings and bird speech; then two other men came from under the tree into the clearing. The first man was like the others. His hair gathered into a tuft on top of his head then spread so that it bobbed as he moved. Tuft went straight to the thorn bushes and began to watch the forest. He also had a bent stick and a twig.

The second man was unlike the others. He was broader and shorter. There was much hair on his body and his head-hair was sleek as if fat had been rubbed in it. The hair lay in a ball at the back of his neck. He had no hair on the front of his head at all so that the sweep of bone skin, daunting in its fungoid pallor, came right over above his ears. Now for the first time, Lok saw the ears of the new men. They were tiny and screwed tightly into the sides of their heads.

Tuft and Chestnut-head were crouching down. They were shifting leaves and blades of grass from the footprints that Fa and Lok had made. Tuft looked up and spoke:

"Tuami."

Chestnut-head followed the prints with outstretched hand. Tuft spoke to the broad man.

"Tuami!"

The broad man turned to them from the pile of stones and sticks which had occupied him. He threw a quick bird-noise, incongruously delicate, and they answered. Fa spoke in Lok's ear.

"It is his name——"

Tuami and the others were bent and nodding over the prints. Where the ground hardened towards the tree the footprints were invisible and when Lok expected the new men to put their noses to the ground they straightened up and stood. Taumi began to laugh. He was pointing towards the fall, laughing and twittering. Then he stopped, struck his palms loudly against each other, said one word and returned to the pile.

As though the one word had changed the clearing, the new men began to relax. Although Chestnut-head and Tuft still watched the forest, they stood, each at a side of the clearing, looking over the thorns and their sticks unbent. Pine-tree did not move any of the bundles for a while; he put one hand to his shoulder, pulled a piece of hide and stepped out of his skin. This hurt Lok like the sight of a thorn under a man's nail; but then he saw that Pine-tree did not mind, was glad in fact, was cool and comfortable in his own white skin. He was naked now like Lok, except that he had a piece of deerskin wound tightly round his thin waist and loins.

Now Lok could see two other things. The new people did not move like anything he had ever seen before. They were balanced on top of their legs, their waists were so wasp-thin that when they moved their bodies swayed backwards and forwards. They did not look at the earth but straight ahead. And they were not merely hungry. Lok knew famine when he saw it. The new people were dying. The flesh was sunken to their bones as Mal's flesh had sunken. Their movements, though they had in their bodies the bending grace of a young bough, were dream-slow. They walked upright and they should be dead. It was as though something that Lok could not see were

133

supporting them, holding up their heads, thrusting them slowly and irresistibly forward. Lok knew that if he were as thin as they, he would be dead already.

Tuft had thrown his skin on the ground below the dead tree and was heaving at a great bundle. Chestnut-head came quickly to help him and they lifted together. Lok saw their faces crease as they laughed at each other and a sudden gush of affection for them pushed the heavy feeling down in his body. He could see how they shared the weight, felt in his own limbs the drag and desperate effort. Tuami came back. He took off his skin, stretched, scratched himself and knelt on the ground. He swept a patch bare of leaves until the brown earth showed. He had a little stick in his right hand and he talked to the other men. There was much nodding. The logs bumped and there was a noise of voices by the water. The men in the clearing stopped talking. Tuft and Chestnut-head began to move round the thorns again.

Then a new man appeared. He was tall and not as thin as the others. The hair under his mouth and above the head was grey and white like Mal's. It frizzed in a cloud and under it a huge cat-tooth hung from either ear. They could not see his face for his back was to them. In their heads they called him the old man. He stood looking down at Tuami and his harsh voice dived and struggled.

Tuami made more marks. They joined; and suddenly Lok and Fa shared a picture of the old woman drawing a line round the body of Mal. Fa's eyes flickered side-ways at Lok and she made a tiny down-stabbing motion with one finger. Those men who were not on watch gathered round Tuami and talked to each other and to the old man. They did not gesticulate much nor dance out their meanings as Lok and Fa might have done but their thin lips puttered and flapped. The old man made a movement with his arm and bent down to Tuami. He said something to him.

Tuami shook his head. The men went a little way from him and sat down in a row with only Tuft still on watch. Fa and Lok watched what Tuami was doing over the row of hairy heads. Tuami scrambled round the other side of the patch and they could see his face. There were upright lines between his eyebrows and the point of his tongue was moving after the line as he drew it. The line of heads began to twitter again. A man picked some small sticks and broke them. He shut them in his hand and each of the others took one from him.

Tuami got up, went to a bundle and pulled out a bag of leather. There were stones and wood, and shapes in it and he arranged them by the mark on the ground. Then he squatted down in front of the men, between them and the marked patch. Immediately the men began to make a noise with their mouths. They struck their hands together and the noise went with the sharp smacks. The noise swept and plunged and twisted yet always remained the same shape, like the hummocks at the foot of the fall that were rushing water yet always the same in the same place. Lok's head began to fill with the fall as though he had looked at it too long and it was sending him to sleep. The tightness of his skin had relaxed a little since he saw the new people liking each other. Now the flock was coming back into his head as the voices and the smack! smack! went on.

The shattering call of a rutting stag blared just under the tree. The flock left Lok's head. The men had bent till their various heads of hair swept the ground. The stag of all stags was dancing out into the clearing. He came round the line of heads, danced to the other side of the marks, turned and stood still. He blared his call again. Then there was silence in the clearing, while the woodpigeons talked to each other.

Tuami became very busy. He began to throw things on to the marks. He reached forward and made important movements. There was colour on the bare patch, colour of autumn leaves, red berries, the white of frost and the dull blackness that fire will leave on rock. The men's hair still lay on the ground and they said nothing.

Tuami sat back.

The skin that had tightened over Lok's body went wintry chill. There was another stag in the clearing. It lay where the marks had been, flat on the ground; it was racing along and yet, like the men's voices and the water below the fall, it stayed in the same place. Its colours were those of the breeding season, but it was very fat, its small dark eye spied Lok's eye through the ivy. He felt caught and cowered down in the soft wood where the food ran and tickled. He did not want to look.

Fa had his wrist and was drawing him up again. Fearfully he put his eye to the leaves and looked back at the flat stag; but it was hidden for men were standing in front of it. Pine-tree was holding a piece of wood in his left hand and it was polished and there was a branch or a piece of a branch sticking out of the farther side of it. One of Pine-tree's fingers was stretched along this branch. Tuami stood opposite him. He took hold of the other end of the wood. Pine-tree was talking to the standing stag and the flat stag. They could hear that he was pleading. Tuami raised his right hand in the air. The stag blared. Tuami struck hard and there was now a glistening stone biting into the wood. Pine-tree stood still for a moment or two. Then he removed his hand carefully from the polished wood and a finger remained stretched out on the branch. He turned away and came to sit with the others. His face was more like bone than it had been before, and he moved very slowly and with a stagger. The other men held up their hands and helped him down among them. He said nothing. Chestnut-head took out some hide and bound up his hand and both the stags waited until he had finished.

Tuami turned the wooden thing over and the finger lingered, then dropped off with a little plop. It lay on the foxy red of the stag. Tuami sat down again. Two of the men had their arms round Pine-tree who was leaning sideways. There was a great stillness so that the fall sounded nearer.

Chestnut-head and Bush stood up and went near the lying stag. They held their curved sticks in one hand and the red-feathered twigs in the other. The standing stag moved his man's hand as though he were sprinkling them with something, then he reached out and touched them each on the cheek with a frond of fern. They began to bend over the stag on the ground, stretching their arms down and their right elbows were rising behind them. Then there was a flick! flick! and two twigs were sticking in the stag by its heart. They bent down, pulled the twigs out and the stag made no movement. The seated men beat their hands together and made the water-hump sounds over and over till Lok yawned and licked his lips. Chestnut-head and Bush were still standing with their sticks. The stag blared, the men bent till their hair was on the ground. The stag began to dance again. His dance prolonged the sound of voices. He came near; he passed under the tree and out of sight and the voices ceased. Behind them, between the dead tree and the river, the stag blared once more.

Tuami and Bush ran quickly to the thorns across the trail and pulled one aside. They stood each side of the opening, pulling back, and Lok could see that now their eyes were shut. Chestnut-head and Bush stole forward softly, their bent sticks raised. They passed through the opening, disappeared noiselessly into the forest and Tuami and Tuft let the thorns fall back.

The sun had moved so that the stag that Tuami had made was smelling at the shadow of the dead tree. Pine-tree was sitting on the ground under the tree and shivering a little. The men began to move slowly in the dream sloth of hunger. The old man came out from under the dead tree and began to talk to Tuami. Now his hair was tied tightly to his head and spots of sun slid over it. He walked forward and looked down at the stag. He reached out a foot and began to rub it round in the stag's body. The stag did nothing but allowed itself to be hidden. In a moment or two there was nothing on the ground but patches of colour and a head with a tiny eye. Tuami turned away, talking to himself, went to a bundle and rummaged. He brought out a spike of bone, heavy and wrinkled at one end like the surface of a tooth and fined down at the other to a blunt point. He knelt and began to rub this blunt point with a little stone and Lok could hear it scrape. The old man came close to him, pointed to the bone, laughed in a roaring voice and pretended to thrust something into his chest. Tuami bent his head and went on rubbing. The old man pointed to the river and then to the ground and began to make a long speech. Tuami thrust the bone and stone into the hide by his waist, got up and passed under the dead tree out of sight.

The old man stopped talking. He sat carefully on a bundle near the centre of the clearing. The stag's head with its tiny eye was at his feet.

Fa spoke in Lok's ear:

"He went away before. He fears the other stag."

Lok had an immediate and vivid picture of the standing stag that had danced and blared. He shook his head in agreement.

EIGHT

Fa shifted herself with great care and settled again. Lok, glancing sideways, saw her red tongue pass along her lips. A pause linked them and for a moment Lok saw two Fas who slid apart and could only be brought together by great firmness. The inside of the ivy was full of flying things that sang thinly or settled on his body so that the skin twitched. The shadows between the bars and patches of sunlight detached themselves and sank until the sunlight was on a different level. Odd sayings of Mal or the old woman swam up with pictures and mixed with the voices of the new people until he hardly knew which was which. It could hardly be the old man below them who was talking in Mal's voice of the summer land where the sun was as warm as a fire and fruit ripened all year long, nor could the overhang mix as it now did with the thorn bushes and bundles of the clearing. The feeling that was so unpleasant had sunk and spread like a pool. Lok was almost used to it.

There was a pain in his wrist. He opened his eyes and looked down irritably. Fa had her fingers round it and his flesh was raised painfully on either side of them. Then quite clearly he heard the new one mew. The bird-chatter and high laughter of the new people was lifted to a new height as though they had all become children. Fa was turning in the tree back to the river. For a while Lok

lay bemused by the sun and his mixture of waking
dreams and new people. Then the new one mewed again
so that Lok himself turned with Fa and peered through
to the river.

One of the two logs was moving in to the bank. Tuami
sat at the back, digging, and the remainder of the log was
full of people. They were women, for he could see their
naked and empty breasts. They were much smaller than
the men and they carried less of the removable fur on
their bodies. Their hair was less astonishing and elab-
orate than the men's. There was a crumpled look about
their faces and they were very thin. Between Tuami and
the bundles and crumpled women sat a creature who
caught Lok's eye so firmly that he had little time to in-
spect the others. She was a woman, too, she carried shining fur round her waist that rose and was looped over
either arm and formed a pouch at the back of her head.
Her hair gleamed black and was arranged round the bone
white of her face like the petals of a flower. Her shoulders
and breast were white, startlingly white by contrast, for
the new one was struggling over them. He was trying to
get away from the water and climbing over her shoulder
to that pouch of fur behind her, and she was laughing,
her face crumpled, mouth open, so that Lok could see
her strange, white teeth. There was too much to see and
he became eyes again that registered and perhaps would
later remember what now he was not aware of. The
woman was fatter than the others, as the old man had
been fatter; but she was not as old as he and there was
milk standing in the points of her breasts. The new one
had hold of her shining hair and was pulling himself up
while she tried to drag him down; her head was leaning

sideways, face up. The laughter rose like the charm of starlings. The log slid under the limit of his spy-hole and Lok heard the bushes sigh by the bank.

He turned to Fa. There was silent laughter in her face and she was shaking her head. She looked at him and he saw that there was water standing in her eyes so full that at any moment it might spill out into the hollows. She stopped laughing; her face crumpled till it looked as though she were bearing the pain of a long thorn in her side. Her lips came together, parted, and though she did not give it breath he knew she had spoken the word.

"Milk——"

The laughter faded and a babble of speech took its place. There were the heavy sounds of things being lifted out of the log and thrown on the bank. Lok stirred another hole into the ivy and looked down. By his side he knew that Fa had already done so.

The fat woman had calmed the new one. She stood by the water and he was sucking her breast. The other women were moving about, pulling at bundles or opening them with clever twists and flutters of their hands. One of them, Lok could see, was only a child, tall and thin, with deerskin wrapped round her waist. She was looking down at a bag that lay on the ground by her feet. One of the other women was opening it. As Lok watched he saw the bag change shape convulsively. The mouth opened, then Liku tumbled out. She fell on all fours, and leapt. He saw that there was a long piece of skin that led from her neck and as she leapt the woman fell on this and grabbed it. Liku turned over in the air and landed on her back with a thump. The starlings charmed again. Liku tugged, ran round, then squatted under the great tree.

Lok could see her round belly and how she was holding the little Oa against it. The woman who had opened the bag led the long skin round the tree and twisted it together. Then she went away. The fat woman moved towards Liku so that Lok could see the shiny top of her head and the thin white line where her hair divided. She spoke to Liku, knelt down, spoke again, laughing and the new one was at her breast. Liku said nothing but moved the little Oa up from her belly to her chest. The woman stood up and went away.

The girl came, hunger-slow, and squatted down about her own length away from Liku. She said nothing but watched her. For a while the two children looked at each other. Liku stirred. She picked something off the tree and put it in her mouth. The girl watched, straight lines appeared between her brows. She shook her head. Lok and Fa looked at each other and shook their heads eagerly. Liku took another piece of fungus from the tree and held it out to the girl, who backed away. Then she came forward, reached gingerly, and snatched the food. She hesitated, put the food to her mouth and began to chew. She looked quickly from side to side at the places where the other women had disappeared, then swallowed. Liku gave her another piece, so small that only children could eat it. The girl swallowed again. Then they were silent and looking at each other.

The girl pointed to the little Oa and asked a question, but Liku said nothing and for a time there was silence. They could see how she examined Liku from head to foot, and perhaps, though they could not see her face, Liku was doing the same. Liku took the little Oa from her chest and balanced her on her shoulder. Suddenly the girl laughed, showing her teeth and then Liku laughed and they were laughing together.

Lok and Fa were laughing too. The feeling in Lok had turned warm and sunny. He felt like dancing were it not for the outside-Lok who insisted on listening for danger.

Fa put her head to his.

"When it is dark we will take Liku and run away."

The fat woman came down to the water. She spread the furs and sat down and they saw that the new one was no longer with her. The furs slid down from her arms till she was naked to the waist, hair and skin gleaming in the sunlight. She lifted her arms to the back of her head, bowed, and began to work at the pattern in her hair. All at once the petals fell in black snakes that hung over her shoulders and breasts. She shook her head like a horse and the snakes flew back till they could see her breasts again. She took thin white thorns out of her head and put them in a little pile by the water. Then she felt in her lap and picked up a piece of bone that was divided like the fingers of a hand. She lifted the hand and passed the bone fingers through her hair again and again till the hair was no longer snakes, but a fall of shining black and the white line lay neatly along the top. She stopped playing with her hair and watched the two girls for a while, speaking to them every now and then. The thin girl was putting twigs together on the ground and joining them at the top. Liku was on all fours, watching her and saying nothing. The fat woman began to work at her hair; she twisted and pulled through, she smoothed, she passed the bone hand here and there, she bowed and ducked; and the hair was building into another pattern that humped up and then coiled close.

Lok heard Tuami speak. The fat woman took her fur quickly and slid it up to her shoulders so that her navel and the wide, white rump was hidden. Her breast only showed and the fur cradled them. She looked sideways under the tree and he knew she was talking to Tuami. She spoke with much laughter.

The old man spoke loudly from the clearing and now that Lok had attention for more than the children he understood how many new sounds there were. Some wood was being broken and a fire was crackling and people were beating things. Not only the old man but the others too were giving orders in their high bird-voices. Lok yawned happily. There would be darkness and a swift flight through the dark with Liku on his back.

Tuami went back under the tree and talked with the old man. Pine-tree came into sight in the back of a log. There was wood piled high in it and in the water behind it swam a group of the heavy logs from the clearing on the island. His shadow was before him now for the sun was just declining from the highest point of its flight through the sky. It blazed up at Lok from the broken water round the logs and made him blink. Pine-tree and the fat woman touched their heads of hair and talked to each other for a moment. Then the old man appeared under Lok and began to gesticulate and talk loudly. The fat woman laughed up at him, her chin lifted, she looked sideways at him and the reflections from the river plucked apart and quivered over her white skin. The old man went away again.

The children were close together. The thin girl was bending over her cave of twigs and Liku was squatting by her as far away from the dead tree as the strip of skin would reach. The thin girl was holding the little Oa in her hands, turning her over and over and examining her curiously. She spoke to Liku then put the little Oa carefully into the cave so that she lay down on her back. Liku gazed at the thin girl with eyes of adoration.

The fat woman stood up, smoothing her furs. She had hung a bright, glittering thing round her neck so that it lay between her breasts. Lok saw that it was one of the pretty, bending yellow stones that the people sometimes picked up and played with until they tired of them and threw them away. The fat woman stepped, swaying on her hips, and passed out of sight into the clearing. Liku was talking to the thin girl. They were pointing at each other.

"Liku!"

The thin girl laughed all over her face. She clapped her hands.

"Liku! Liku!"

She pointed to her own chest.

"Tanakil."

Liku regarded her solemnly.

"Liku."

The thin girl was shaking her head and Liku was shaking her head.

"Tanakil."

Liku spoke very carefully.

"Tanakil."

The thin girl leapt to her feet, shouted and clapped and laughed. One of the crumpled women came and stood looking down at Liku. Tanakil jabbered at her, pointed, nodding, then stopped and spoke to Liku carefully.

"Tanakil."

146

Liku screwed up her face.

"Tanakil."

They all three laughed. Tanakil went to the dead tree, examined it, talked, and picked off a piece of the yellow fungus that Liku had given her. She put it in her mouth. The crumpled woman screamed so that Liku fell over. The crumpled woman struck Tanakil's shoulder fiercely, screaming and shouting. Tanakil quickly put her hand to her mouth and pulled the fungus out. The woman smacked it out of her hand so that it fell in the river. She screamed at Liku who bolted back to the tree. The woman bent down to her, keeping out of reach and made fierce noices at her.

"Ah!" she said. "Ah!"

She turned on Tanakil, talking all the time and pushed her with one hand while she kept the other on her hip. She pushed and talked, urging Tanakil towards the clearing. Tanakil moved unwillingly, looking back. Then she too was out of sight. Liku crept to the cave of twigs, snatched up the little Oa and scuttled back to the tree again with the little Oa at her chest. The crumpled woman came back and looked at her. Some of the crumples smoothed out of her face. For a time she said nothing. Then she bent down, keeping the length of the skin away from Liku.

"Tamakil."

Liku did not move. The woman picked up a twig and held it out gingerly. Liku took it doubtfully, smelt it and dropped it on the ground. The woman spoke again.

"Tanakil?"

The woodpigeons talked for answer and the water light shivered up and down the woman's face.

147

"Tanakil!"

Liku said nothing. Presently the woman went away.

Fa took her hand from Lok's mouth.

"Do not speak to her."

She frowned at him. The twitching of his skin diminished now that the woman was no longer near Liku. Outside-Lok reminded him to be careful.

There were raised voices in the clearing. Lok and Fa shifted round again. They could see great alterations. A good bright fire burned in the centre and its heavy smoke went straight up into the sky. There were caves built on either side of the clearing, overhangs of branches that the new people had brought with them in their logs. Most of the bundles had disappeared so that there was plenty of room near the fire. The people were gathered there and they were all talking. They were facing the old man who was talking back. They held out their arms to him all except Tuami who was standing to one side as though he were of a different people. The old man was shaking his head and shouting. The people turned inwards until they were a knot of backs and they muttered to each other. Then they were at the old man again, shouting. He shook his head, turned his back on them and bent into the overhang on the left. The people swarmed round Tuami, shouting still. He held up one hand and they were silent. He pointed to the stag's head that still lay on the ground, sticking out beyond the logs of the fire. He jerked his head at the forest, while the people clamoured again. The old man came out of the cave and held up a hand like Tuami. The people stilled for a moment.

The old man said one word, very loudly. Immediately there was a great shout from the people. Even their slow movements quickened a little. The fat woman brought a curious bundle out of the cave. It was the whole skin of an animal but it wobbled as if the animal were made of water. The people brought hollow pieces of wood and held them under the animal which immediately made water in them. It filled each, for Lok could see the water flash when it fell in the wood. The fat woman was happy with the animal as she had been happy with the new one; all the people were happy, even the old man who grinned and laughed. The people carried their pieces of wood away to the fire, carefully holding them so that they would not spill, though there was much water in the river. They knelt or sat slowly and put the wood to their mouths and drank. Tuami knelt down grinning, by the fat woman, and the animal made water in his mouth. Fa and Lok cowered down in the tree with twisted faces. A lump was going up and down in Lok's throat. The food of the tree crawled over him and he grimaced as he absently popped them one after another in his mouth. He licked his lips, grimaced, and yawned again. Then he looked down at Liku.

The thin girl was back again. She smelt different, sour, but she was cheerful. She began to talk to Liku in the high bird language and presently Liku came a little way from the tree. Tanakil looked sideways to where the people were gathered round the fire, then came softly to Liku. She laid a hand on the strip of skin where it led round the trunk and began to untwist it. The strip came free. Tanakil twisted it round her wrist, making diving and turning movements like the summer flight of a swallow. She walked right round the tree and the strip came with her. She spoke to Liku, tugged gently and the two girls moved away together.

Tanakil talked all the time. Liku kept close to her and listened with both ears for they could see them twitch. Lok had to stir another hole to see where they went. Tanakil took Liku to look at a bundle.

Sleepily Lok changed his viewpoint until he could see the clearing. The old man was walking about restlessly and he held the grey hair under his mouth with one hand. Those people who were not on guard or arranging the fire were lying down, looking flat as dead men. The fat woman had gone into a cave again.

The old man decided something. Lok could see how his hand came away from his face. He clapped his hands loudly and began to speak. The men who were lying by the fire got up unwillingly. The old man was pointing to the river, urging them. There was silence from the men and then a great shaking of heads and sudden speech. The old man's voice became angry. He walked towards the water, stopped, spoke over his shoulder and pointed to the hollow logs. Slowly the dream men came forward over the tufts of grass and leafy earth. They talked softly to themselves and each other. The old man began to shout as the woman had shouted at Tanakil. The dream men came to the river bank and stood looking into the logs without movement or speech. The sour smell of the drink from the wobbling animal rose up to Lok like the decay of autumn. Tuami walked across the clearing and stood behind them.

The old man made a speech. Tuami, nodding went away, and a few moments later Lok heard chopping noises. The two other men took the strips of hide from the bushes, jumped into the water, pushed the back end of the first log out into the river and brought the other to the bank. They stood on either side of the end and began to lift. Then they both bowed into the log, gasping. The old man shouted again with both hands high in the air. Then he pointed. The men heaved again. Tuami came with a piece of a branch that was smoothly trimmed. The men began to tear away the soft earth of the bank. Lok turned round in his nest to look for Liku. He could see that Tanakil was showing her all manner of wonderful things, a line of sea shells that hung on a thread and an Oa so lifelike that at first Lok thought it was only asleep or perhaps dead. She held the strip of skin in her hand but it was slack, for Liku was keeping close to the bigger girl, looking up as she looked at Lok when he swung her or clowned for her. The straight lines of sunlight were slanting into the clearing from over the gap. The old man began to shout and at his voice the women came crawling and yawning out of the caves. He shouted again so that they shambled under the tree talking to each other as the men had done. Soon there was no one in sight but the guard and the two children.

A new sort of shouting started between the tree and the river. Lok turned round to see what was happening.

"A-ho! A-ho! A-ho!"

The new people, men and women, were leaning back. The log was looking at them, its snout resting on the log that Tuami had brought. Lok knew that this end was its snout because the log had eyes on either side. He had not seen them before because they had been under the white stuff which was now darkend and half washed off. The people were joined to the log by strips of skin. The old man was urging them and they leaned back, gasping, their feet pushing lumps of earth out of the soft ground.

They moved jerkily and the log followed them, watching all the time. Lok could see the lines in their faces and the sweat as they passed under the tree and out of sight. The old man followed them and the shouting went on.

Tanakil and Liku came back to the tree. Liku was holding Tanakil's wrist with one hand and the little Oa with the other. The shouting stopped and all the people trudged gloomily into sight and lined up by the river. Tuami and Pine-tree got into the water by the second log. Tanakil walked forward to see but Liku pulled away from her. Tanakil explained to her but Liku would not go near the water. Tanakil began to pull the strip of skin. Liku held on to the earth with hands and feet. Suddenly Tanakil began to scream at her like the crumple-faced woman. She picked up a stick, spoke in a biting sharp voice and began to pull again. Liku still held on and Tanakil hit her across the back with the stick. Liku howled and Tanakil pulled and beat.

"A-ho! A-ho! A-ho!"

The second log had its snout on the bank but this time it did not climb any further. It slipped back and the people fell over. The old man shouted at the top of his voice. He pointed furiously down the river, then at the fall, then into the forest and his voice raved all the time. The people shouted back at him. Tanakil stopped hitting Liku and watched the grown-ups. The old man was moving round stirring the people with his foot. Tuami was standing to one side, watching him like a log and saying nothing. Slowly the people got to their feet and laid hold of the strips again. Tanakil lost interest, turned away and knelt by Liku. She picked up small stones, threw them in the air and tried to catch them on the narrow back of her hand. Soon Liku was watching her again. The log climbed out on the bank, wagged and was firmly ashore. The people leant back and moved out of sight.

Lok looked down on Liku, happy in the sight of her round belly and the quiet now that Tanakil was no longer using her stick. He thought of the new one at the fat woman's breast and smiled sideways at Fa. Fa grinned at him wryly. She did not seem to be as happy as he was. The feeling inside him had sunk away and disappeared like the frost when the sun finds it on a flat rock. The people who were so miraculously endowed with possessions no longer seemed to him the immediate menace they had been earlier. Even outside-Lok was lulled and not so sharp on sounds and smells. He yawned hugely and pressed his palms into his eye-sockets. The flock was swarming, drifting along as when in high summer a wind cards it out of the bushes of the plain and the air is full of drifting streamers. He could hear Fa whispering outside him.

"Remember that we shall take them when it is dark."

A picture came to him of the fat woman laughing and giving milk.

"How will you feed him?"

"I will half-eat for him. And perhaps the milk will come."

He thought of this. Fa spoke once more.

"Presently the new people will sleep."

The new people were not yet asleep or anything near it. They were making more noise than ever. Both logs were in the clearing, lying across thick, round branches. The people were grouped round the last one and screaming at the old man. He was pointing fiercely at the way into the forest and making his bird-noises flutter and twist. The people were shaking their heads, freeing themselves from the lines of skin, moving away towards the caves. The old man was shaking his fists at the sky where the air was darkest blue, was beating his head with his fists; but the people moved in their dream of walking to the fire and the caves. When he was quite alone by the trunks of wood he fell silent. There was the beginning of darkness under the trees and the sunlight was lifting from the ground.

The old man walked very slowly towards the river. Then he stopped and they could see no expression on his face, but he went back quickly to his cave and disappeared inside. Lok heard the fat woman speak and then the old man came out. He walked towards the river slowly, in the same footsteps, and this time he did not pause by the logs but came straight on. He passed under the tree, stood between the tree and the river, looking down at the children.

Tanakil was teaching Liku to catch, the stick forgotten. When she saw the old man she stood up, put her hands behind her and rubbed one foot over the other. Liku did this too as well as she could. The old man said nothing for a while. Then he jerked his head at the clearing and spoke sharply. Tanakil took the end of the strip of skin in her hand and walked under the tree with Liku following. Turning carefully in the tree, Lok saw them go into a cave. When he looked back on the river side the old man was standing and making water over the edge of the bank. The sunlight had left the river and was caught in the treetops on the other side. There was a great redness over the fall and the gap and the water sounded very loud. The old man came back to the tree, stood under it and peered carefully towards the thorns where the guard was standing. Then he went to the other side of the tree and looked again, and all round. He came back, and leaned against the tree facing the water. He put his hand inside the skin of his chest and pulled out a lump. Lok smelt, saw and recognized. The old man was eating the meat that had been intended for Liku. They could hear him as he leaned there, head bent, elbows out, tearing, pulling and chewing. He sounded busy at his meat as a beetle in dead wood.

Someone was coming. Lok heard him but the old man, caught between the sounds of his two jaws, did not. The man came round the tree, saw the old man, stopped, howled with fury. It was Pine-tree. He ran back to the clearing, stood by the fire and began to shout at the top of his voice. Figures pulled themselves out of the dark caves, men and women. The darkness was swarming over the ground and Pine-tree kicked the fire so that sparks and flames shot up. Then there was a flood of firelight to wrestle with the swarm of darkness under the still, bright sky. The old man was shouting by the logs; Pine-tree was shouting and pointing at him and the fat woman came out of a cave with the new one squirming over her shoulder. All at once the people made a rush. The old man jumped into one of the logs, picked up a wooden leaf and brandished it. The fat woman began to scream at the people and the noise was so great that birds flapped in the trees. Now the old man's voice had the dusk to itself. The people were a little quieter. Tuami who had said nothing, but stood by the fat woman, said something now and the people took up and repeated what he said. Their voices were louder again. The old man was pointing at the stag's head where it lay by the fire but the noise of the people saying one word over and over again sounded as if they were coming nearer. The fat woman ducked into her cave and Lok could see the people fasten their eyes on the entrance. She came out not with the new one but with the animal that wobbled. At this the people shouted and clapped their hands. They moved away quickly and brought the hollow pieces of wood and the animal on the fat woman's shoulder made water into them. The people drank and Lok could see how the bones of their throats moved in the firelight. The old man was waving them back to their caves but they would not go. They came back to the fat woman and got more to drink. The fat woman was not laughing now but looking from the old man to the people and then to Tuami. He was close to her and his face was smiling. The fat woman tried to take the animal back into the cave but Pine-tree and a woman would not let her. At that the old man rushed forward and the knot of them began to struggle together. Tuami stood by the struggle watching as though the people were something he had drawn in the air with his stick. More of the people joined in. The crowd was turning round and round and the fat woman was screaming. The wobbling animal slid off her shoulder and disappeared. Some of the people fell on top of it. Lok heard a watery sound and then the heap of people sank a little. They staggered apart and there was the animal flat on the ground, flat as the stag that Tuami had made, but far more dead-looking.

The old man made himself very tall.

Lok yawned. These sights would not join together. His eyes closed, jerked open. The old man had both arms stretched up in the air. He was facing the people and the voice he used was frightening them. They had moved a little back. The fat woman sneaked into a cave. Tuami had disappeared. The old man's voice rose, finished, his hands fell. There was silence and fear and a sour smell from the dead animal.

For a while the people said nothing but stayed, crouched a little, leaning away. Suddenly one of the women rushed forward. She screamed up at the old man, she rubbed her belly, she held out her breasts for him to look at, she spat at him. The people began to move again. There was nodding and shouting. The old man shouted the others down and pointed to the head of the stag. Then there was silence. The people's eyes turned in and down to the stag that still watched Lok with its little eye through the spy-hole.

There was a noise in the forest outside the clearing. Gradually the people became aware of it. Someone was howling. The thorns moved, opened; Chestnut-head, blood glistening all down his left leg, hopped through, holding on to Bush. When he saw the fire, he lay down, and a woman ran to him. Bush came forward towards the people.

Lok's eyelids fell and bounced open again. For a dreamy moment he saw himself in a picture telling all this to Liku who would not understand it any more than he did.

The fat woman appeared by the cave and she had the new one sucking at her breast. Bush was asking a question. A shout answered him. The woman who had held out her empty breast was pointing to the old man, the dead tree, and to the people. Chestnut-head spat at the stag's head and the people shouted again, moving forward. The old man lifted up his hands and began that same high, menacing speech but the people jeered and laughed. Chestnut-head stood by the stag's head. They could see his eyes gleaming in the firelight like two stones. He began to draw a twig from his waist and he held the bent stick in his other hand. He and the old man watched each other.

The old man took a step sideways and talked rapidly. He reached the fat woman, put out his hands and tried to take the new one from her. She bent quickly and snapped at his hand with her mouth as any woman would, so that the old man danced and howled. Chestnut-head put the twig across the bent stick and pulled the red feathers back. The old man stopped dancing and went towards him, hands out, palms facing the twig. He stood still almost within reach of Chestnut-head, curled the fingers of his right hand all except the long one. This one he moved sideways until it was pointing at one of the caves. All the people were very silent. The fat woman laughed in a high voice and was still again. Tuami was watching the old man's back. The old man glanced round the clearing, peered out to where the darkness was crowded under the trees and then back at the people. None of them said anything.

Lok yawned and backed down into the hollow of the treetop where he was protected from the sight of the people and their whole camp was nothing but a flicker of reflected light over the trees. He looked up at Fa, inviting her to sleep at his side but she did not notice him.

He could see her face and her eyes peering through the ivy and unblinkingly open. So concentrated was she that even when he touched her leg with his hand she did nothing but went on staring. He saw her mouth open and her breathing quicken. She gripped the rotten wood of the dead trunk so that it crunched and crumbled into wet pulp. Despite his tiredness this interested Lok and frightened him a little. He had a picture of one of the people climbing the tree, so he struggled back and began to stir the leaves open. Fa glanced sideways quickly and her face was like the face of a sleeper who wrestles with a terrible dream. She grabbed his wrist and forced him down. She gripped him by the shoulders and burrowed her face against his chest. Lok put his arm round her and outside-Lok felt a warm pleasure in the touch. But Fa had no wish to play. She knelt up again, pulled him towards her and held his head against her breast while her face looked downwards through the leaves and her heart beat urgently against his cheek. He tried to see what it was that made her so afraid but when he struggled she held him close and all he could see was the angle of her jaw and her eyes, open, open for ever, watching.

The flock came back and her body was warm. Lok yielded, knowing that she would wake him when the people slept and they could run away with the children. He burrowed close, holding, pillowed over the thumping heart with the tight arms round him so that the flock, swarming now in the darkness became a whole world of exhausted sleep.

NINE

He awoke to fight with arms that were pressing him down, arms holding his shoulder and a hand smothering his face. He talked and bubbled against the fingers, ready almost to bite them from the new habit of terror. Fa's face was close to his and she was holding him down as he threshed against the leaves and moulded tinder wood.

"Quiet!"

She had spoken louder than ever before in the tree, had spoken in more than an ordinary voice as though the people were no longer all round them. He ceased to struggle and was properly awake, noticing how the light was leaping over the dark leaves making spots in their darkness that jumped this way and that together. There were many stars over the tree and they were small and dying by contrast. Sweat was streaming down Fa's face and the skin of her body where he touched it was wet. As he noticed her he heard the new people also for they were noisy as a pack of wolves in cry. They were shouting, laughing, singing, babbling in their bird speech, and the flames of their fire were leaping madly with them. He turned over and poked his fingers into the leaves to see what was happening.

The clearing was full of firelight. They had pulled ashore the great logs that had swum across the river behind Pine-tree and stood them on end over the fire so that they leaned against each other. There was nothing warm and comfortable about this fire—it was like the fall, like a cat. He could see part of the log that had killed Mal leaning against the pile and the hard, ear-like fungi were red hot. The flames came squirting out of the top of the pile as though they were being squeezed from below, they were red and yellow and white and they shot small sparks straight up out of sight. The tops of the flames where they faded out were level with Lok and the blue smoke round them was almost invisible. From the pile with its fountain of flame, light beat round the clearing, not warm light but fierce, white-red and blinding. This light pulsed like a heart so that even the trees round the clearing with their drifts of curling leaves seemed to jump sideways like the holes between the leaves of ivy.

The people were like the fire, made of yellow and white, for they had thrown off their furs and wore nothing but the binding of skin round their waists and loins. They jumped sideways in time with the trees and their hair was fallen or awry so that Lok could not easily tell the difference between the men among them. The fat woman was leaning against one of the hollow logs, her hands braced on either side of her and she was naked to the waist so that her body was yellow and white. Her head was back, throat curved, mouth open and laughing while her loose hair swung down into the hollow of the log. Tuami was crouched by her, his face against her left wrist; and he was moving, not only jerkily back and forth with the fire-light but up, his mouth creeping, his fingers playing, moving up as though he were eating her flesh, moving up towards her naked shoulder. The old man was lying in the other hollow log, his feet sticking out either side. He held a round stone thing in his hand which he put to his mouth every now and then and in between whiles he was singing. The other men and women were scattered round the clearing. They held more of these round stones and now Lok saw that they were drinking from them. His nose caught the scent of what they drank. It was sweeter and fiercer than the other water, it was like the fire and the fall. It was a bee-water, smelling of honey and wax and decay, it drew toward and repelled, it frightened and excited like the people themselves. There were other stones nearer the fire with holes in their tops and the smell seemed to come particularly strongly from them. Now Lok saw that when the people had finished their drink they came to these and lifted them and took more to drink. The girl Tanakil was lying in front of one of the caves, flat on her back as if she were dead. A man and a woman were fighting and kissing and screeching and another man was crawling round and round the fire like a moth with a burnt wing. Round and round he went, crawling, and the other people took no notice of him but went on with their noise.

Tuami had reached the fat woman's neck. He was pulling her and she was laughing and shaking her head and squeezing his shoulder with her hand. The old man sang and the people fought, the man crawled round the fire, Tuami burrowed at the fat woman and all the time the clearing jumped back and forth, sideways.

There was plenty of light for Lok to see Fa. The jerking tired his eyes for they tried to follow it, so he turned his head and looked at her instead. She too was jerking but not so much; and apart from the light her face was

162

very still. Her eyes looked as though they had neither blinked nor shifted since before he fell asleep. The pictures in his head came and went like the firelight. They meant nothing and they began to spin till his head felt as if it would split. He found words for his tongue but his tongue hardly knew how to use them.

"What is it?"

Fa did not move. A kind of half-knowledge, terrible in its very formlessness, filtered into Lok as though he were sharing a picture with her but had no eyes inside his head and could not see it. The knowledge was something like that sense of extreme peril that outside-Lok had shared with her earlier; but this was for inside-Lok and he had no room for it. It pushed into him, displacing the comfortable feeling of after sleep, the pictures and their spinning, breaking down the small thoughts and opinions, the feeling of hunger and the urgency of thirst. He was possessed by it and did not know what it was.

Fa turned her head sideways slowly. The eyes with their twin fires came round like the eyes of the old woman moving up through the water. A movement round her mouth—not a grimace or preparation for speech—set her lips fluttering like the lips of the new people; and then they were open again and still.

"Oa did not bring them out of her belly."

At first the words had no picture connected with them but they sank into the feeling and reinforced it. Then Lok peered through the leaves again for the meaning of the words and he was looking straight at the fat woman's mouth. She was coming towards the tree, holding on to Tuami, and she staggered and screeched with laughter so that he could see her teeth. They were not broad and

163

useful for eating and grinding; they were small and two were longer than the others. They were teeth that remembered wolf.

The fire collapsed with a roar and a torrent of sparks. The old man was no longer drinking but lying still in the hollow log and the other people were sitting or flat and the singing noise was dying like the fire. Tuami and the fat woman passed erratically under the tree and disappeared so that Lok moved round to watch them. The fat woman made for the water but Tuami caught her arm and pulled her round. They stood like that looking at each other, the fat woman pale on one side from the moon, ruddy on the other from the fire. She laughed up at Tuami and stuck her tongue out while he spoke quickly to her. Suddenly he grabbed her with both hands and pulled her against his chest and they wrestled, gasping without speech. Tuami shifted his grip, got her by a hank of long hair and dragged it down till her face lifted, contorted with pain. She stuck the nails of her right hand into his shoulder and dragged down as her hair was dragged. Tuami thrust his face against hers and lurched so that one knee was behind her. He shifted his hand up until it was gripping the back of her head. The hand that was gripped into the flesh of his shoulder slackened, fumbled, reached round him and suddenly they were bound together, straining together, loins against loins and mouth against mouth. The fat woman began to slide down so that Tuami was bending over. He fell clumsily on one knee and her arms were round his neck. She lay back in the moonlight, her eyes shut, her body limp and her breast moving up and down. Tuami was kneeling and fumbling in the fur about her waist. He made a kind of snarling sound and threw himself upon her. Now Lok could see the wolf teeth again. The fat woman was moving her face from side to side and it was contorted as it had been when she struggled against Tuami.

He turned back to Fa. She was still kneeling, looking out into the clearing at the red-hot heap of wood and the sweat on her skin glistened faintly. He had a sudden and brilliant picture of himself and Fa taking the children and racing away through the clearing. He became alert. He put his head by her mouth and whispered.

"Shall we take the children now?"

She leaned away from him so that she was far enough off to see him clearly in the now dim light. She shuddered suddenly as though the moonlight that fell on the tree were wintry.

"Wait!"

The two people beneath the tree were making noises fiercely as though they were quarrelling. In particular the fat woman had begun to hoot like an owl and Lok could hear Tuami gasping like a man who fights with an animal and does not think he will win. He looked down at them and saw that Tuami was not only lying with the fat woman but eating her as well for there was black blood running from the lobe of her ear.

Lok was excited. He reached out and laid a hand on Fa but she had only to turn her eyes of stone upon him and she was immediately surrounded by that same incomprehensible feeling, that worse than Oa feeling which he recognized but could not understand. He took his hand hurriedly from her body and began to stir with it in the leaves until he had a spy-hole that looked at the fire and the clearing. Most of the people had gone into the caves. The old man's feet were the only part of him that was to be seen resting on the sides of the hollow logs. The man who had crawled round the fire was lying on his face among the round stones that held the bee-water, and the hunter who had been on guard was still standing by the thorn fence, leaning on a stick. As Lok watched, this man began to slip down the stick until he collapsed near the thorns and lay still with the moonlight gleaming dully on his bare skin. Tanakil had gone and the crumpled women with her so that the clearing was little but a space round a dull red heap of wood.

He turned round and looked down at Tuami and the fat woman who had risen to a rowdy climax and now lay still, glistening with sweat and smelling of flesh and the honey from the stones. He glanced at Fa who was still silent and terrible and who looked at a picture that was not there in the darkness of the ivy. He dropped his eyes and automatically began to feel over the rotten wood for something to eat. But suddenly as he did so he discovered his thirst and once discovered it would not be ignored. Restlessly he peered down at Tuami and the fat woman for of all the astonishing and inexplicable events that had taken place in the clearing they were at once the most understandable and at the same time the most interesting.

Their fierce and wolflike battle was ended. They had fought it seemed against each other, consumed each other rather than lain together so that there was blood on the woman's face and the man's shoulder. Now, the fighting done and peace restored between them, or whatever state it was that was restored, they played together. Their play was complicated and engrossing. There was no animal on the mountain or the plain, no lithe and able creature of the bushes or forest that had the subtlety and imagination to invent games like these, nor the leisure and incessant wakefulness to play them. They hunted down pleasure as the wolves will follow and run down horses; they seemed to follow the tracks of the invisible prey, to listen, head tilted, faces concentrated and withdrawn in the pale light for the first steps of its secret approach. They sported with their pleasure when they had it fast, as a fox will play with the fat bird she has caught, postponing the death because she has the will to put off and enjoy twice over the pleasure of eating. They were silent now except for little grunts and gasps and an occasional gurgle of secret laughter from the fat woman.

A white owl swept over the tree and a moment later Lok heard his note that always sounded farther away than it was. The sight of Tuami and the fat woman was not as rousing as it had been when they fought together and they were powerless to put down the presence of his thirst. He dared not speak to Fa not only because of her strange remoteness but also because Tuami and the fat woman made so little noise now that speech was dangerous again. He became restless to take the children and run.

The fire was a very dull red and its light hardly reached to the wall of branches buds and twigs round the clearing so that they had begun to be a pattern of darkness against the brighter sky behind them. The ground of the clearing was so sunken in gloom that Lok had to use his night sight to see it. The fire was isolated and seemed to float. Tuami and the fat woman came from beneath the tree unsteadily and they did not walk together but made their way waist deep in shadows to separate caves. Now the fall roared and the voices of the forest, crepitations and scuttering of unseen feet were audible. Another white owl drifted through the clearing and away across the river.

Lok turned to Fa and whispered.

"Now?"

She came close. There was in her voice the same urgency and command as when she had bidden him obey her on the terrace.

"I shall take the new one and jump the thorns. When I have gone, follow."

Lok thought but no picture would come.

"Liku——"

Her hands tightened on his body.

"Fa says 'Do this!'"

He moved quickly so that the ivy leaves brushed each other harshly.

"But Liku——"

"I have many pictures in my head."

Her hands left him. He lay in the treetop and all the pictures of the day began to spin once more. He heard her breathing pass by him and sink into the ivy that rustled again so that he looked quickly into the clearing, but no one stirred. He could just make out the old man's feet sticking out of the hollow log and the holes of deep black where the branch caves were. The fire floated, dull red for the most part, but with a brighter heart where blue flames wandered over the wood. Tuami came out of the cave, stood by the fire, looking down at it. Fa was already half out of the ivy and clinging to the thick branches in the river side of the tree. Tuami took a branch and began to rake the hot ashes together so that they sparkled and sent up a puff of smoke and winking points. The crumpled woman crept out and took the branch from him and for a moment or two they stood swaying and talking. Tuami went away into a cave and the moment after Lok heard a crash as he fell among dry leaves. He waited for the woman to go; but first she dug earth round the fire until there was nothing but a black hummock with a glowing mouth at the top. She carried a sod to the fire and dumped it on the mouth so that the grass flared and crackled while a wave of light shook out over the clearing. She stood, quivering at the end of her long shadow, the light faltered and went out. He half heard, half sensed her as she went feeling towards the cave, fell on hands and knees and crawled inside.

His night-sight came back to him. The clearing was very still again and he heard the noise of Fa's skin scraping against the old bark of the tree as she let herself down. An immediacy of danger came to him; the knowledge that they were about to cheat these strange people and all their inscrutable works, the awful knowledge of Fa creeping towards them caught him by the throat so that he could not breathe and his heart began to shake him. He gripped the rotten wood and cowered behind the ivy with his eyes shut, seeking without knowing for those hours when the dead tree was relatively safe. The scent of Fa rose up to him from the fireward side of the tree and he shared a picture with her of a cave with a great bear standing at the mouth of it. The scent ceased to rise, the picture disappeared and he knew that she had become eyes and ears and nose crawling noiselessly towards the cave by the fire.

His heart slowed a little and his breathing so that he could look again at the clearing. The moon soared from the edge of a thick cloud and poured a grey blue light over the forest. He could see Fa, flattened by the light, clutched down to the ground and not more than twice her length from the dark mound of the fire. The cloud was succeeded by another and the clearing was full of darkness. Over by the thorns that blocked the entry to the trail he heard the guard choke and struggle to his feet. There came the sound of vomiting and then a long moan. Feelings mixed themselves in Lok. He had a half-thought that the new people might choose suddenly to be as they were; to stand up, talk and be wary or infinitely knowing and secure in their strength. With this was mixed a picture of Fa not daring to run first across the log by the terrace; and this feeling of warmth and urgent desire to be with her was part of it. He moved in the ivy cup, parted the leaves towards the river and felt for the branches on the trunk. He let himself down quickly before the feelings had time to change and make an obedient Lok of him; he stood in the long grass at the foot of the dead tree. Now the thought of Liku possessed him and he crept past the tree and tried to see which cave contained her. Fa was moving towards the cave on the right of the fire. Lok moved to the left, he sank on all fours and crept towards the cave that had grown beyond the logs and the pile of unsorted bundles. The hollow logs were lying where the people had left them as though they too had drunk of the honey drink and the old man's feet still stuck out of the nearer one. Lok cowered under the height of the log and sniffed cautiously at the foot above him. It had no toes or rather—now he was able to get so close to it—it was covered in hide like the peoples' waists and it smelt strongly of cow and sweat. Lok lifted his eyes above his nose and looked over the edge of the log. The old man was lying full length in it, his mouth open, and he was snoring through his thin, pointed nose. The hair prickled on Lok's body and he ducked down as though the old man's eyes had been open. He cowered in the torn earth and grass by the log, and now that his nose was adjusted to the old man, it discounted him, for there were many other bits of information coming to it. The logs, for example, were connected with the sea. The white on their sides was sea-white, bitter and evocative of beaches and the ceaseless progression of the waves. There was the smell of pine-tree gum, of a peculiarly thick and fiery sort of mud that his nose could identify as different but not name. There were the smells of many men and women and children and, finally, most obscurely but none the less powerfully, there was the smell compounded of many that had sunk beneath the threshold of separate identification into the one smell of extreme age.

Lok stilled his flesh and the pricking of his hair and crawled along by the log until he came to where the round stones had been left a little way from the hot but lightless fire. They maintained their own atmosphere, a smell so powerful that his mind could see it like a glow or a cloud round the holes in the top. The smell was like the new people, it repelled and attracted, it daunted and enticed, it was like the fat woman and at the same time like the terror of the stag and the old man. Lok was reminded of the stag so strongly that he cowered again; but he could not remember where the stag had gone nor where it came from except that it approached the clearing from behind the dead tree. He turned then, looked up and saw the dead tree with its ivy, vast, shock-headed and impending from the clouds like a cave-bear. He crawled quickly to the hut on the left. The guard over by the thorns groaned again.

Lok smelt his way along the leaning branches at the back of the cave and found a man and a man and another man. There was no smell of Liku unless a sort of generalized smell in his nostrils so faint as to be nothing but an awareness might be connected with her. Wherever he cast over the ground the awareness persisted and would not be tracked down to a source. He grew bold. He gave up his random and fruitless casting and made for the open side of the cave. First the people had set up two sticks and laid one other long stick across the top. Then they had leaned innumerable branches against the long stick so that they formed a leafy overhang in the clearing. There were three of these, one to the left, one to the right, and one between the fire and the thorns where the guard was. The cut ends of the branches had been forced into the earth in a curving line. Lok crawled to the end of the line and put his head round it cautiously. The noise of breathing and snoring that came from the shapes inside was irregular and loud. Someone was asleep not an arm's length from his face. The someone grunted, belched, turned and an arm fell over so that the open palm of the hand brushed Lok's face. He jerked back, quivering, then leant forward and smelt the hand. It was pale, glistening slightly, helpless and innocent as Mal's hand. But it was narrower and longer and of a different colour in its fungoid whiteness.

There was a narrow space between the arm and the place where the ends of the branches slanted into the earth. The picture of Liku so maddeningly present and so hidden drove him forward. He did not know what this feeling required him to do but knew that he must do something. He began to draw his body forward slowly into the narrow space like a snake sliding into a hole. He felt breath on his face and froze. There was a face not a hand's length from his own. He could feel the tickle of the fantastic hair, could see the long, useless cliff of bony skull that prolonged the head above the eyebrows. He could see the dull gleam of an eye beneath a lid that was not tightly shut, see the irregular wolf's teeth, feel now the honey-sour breath on his cheek. Inside-Lok shared a picture of terror with Fa but outside-Lok was coldly brave and still as ice.

Lok passed his arm over the sleeping man and felt space, then leaves and earth on the other side. He put the palm of his hand firmly in the space and prepared to pass his body over on hand and foot, arching away from the sleeper. As he did so the man spoke. The words were deep in his throat as though he had no tongue and they interfered with his breathing. His chest began to rise and fall quickly. Lok whipped his arm back and crouched again. The man threshed about in the leaves; his clenched fist smacked a shower of lights out of Lok's eye. Lok shrank back and the man arched so that his belly was higher than his head. All the time the tongueless words were struggling and the arms beat about among the sloping branches. The man's head turned to Lok and he could see that his eyes were staring wide open, staring at nothing, turning with the head like the eyes of the old woman in the water. They looked through him and the fear contracted on his skin. The man was jerking his body higher and higher, the words had become a series of croaks that grew louder and louder. There was a noise coming from one of the other huts, the shrill chatter of women and then a terrified screech. The man by Lok fell over on his side, staggered up and struck away the branches so that they fell in a pile. The man staggered forward and his croaks became a shout that someone answered. Other men were struggling in the cave, knocking down the boughs and shouting. By the thorns the guard was stumbling round and fighting with shadows. A figure stood up out of the wreckage by Lok, saw the first man dimly and swung a great stick at him. All at once the darkness of the clearing was full of people who fought and screamed. Someone was kicking the sods of earth away from the fire so that a dim glow and then a burst of flame lit up the crowded ground and ring of trees. The old man was standing there, his grey hair swirling round his head and face. Fa was there, running and empty-handed. She saw the old man and swerved. A figure by Lok swung a huge stick with so much purpose that Lok grabbed it. Then he was rolling with a tangle of limbs and teeth and claws. He pulled away and the tangle went on fighting and snarling. He saw Fa rise and dive at the top of the thorns and vanish over them, saw the old man, a demented picture of hair and gleaming eyes, swing a stick with a lump on the end into the heap of struggling men. As Lok flung himself over the thorns he saw the guard fighting to get through them. He landed on his hands and ran till bushes clutched at him. He saw the guard fly past, with bent stick and twig ready, duck under the curved bough of a beech tree and disappear into the forest.

There was a fire burning brightly now in the clearing. The old man was standing by it and the other men were picking themselves up. The old man shouted and pointed until one of the men staggered to the thorns and ran after the guard. The women were crowding round the old man and the child Tanakil was among them with the backs of her hands to her eyes. The two men came running back, shouted at the old man and fought their way through the thorns into the clearing. Now Lok could see that the women were throwing branches on the fire, the branches that had made them a cave. The fat woman was there, twisting one hand over the other and wailing with the new one on her shoulder. Tuami was talking urgently to the old man, pointing to the forest and then down at the ground where the stag's head was. The fire grew; whole sprays of leaves burst into light with an explosive crackle so that the trees of the clearing were to be seen as clearly as by day. The people crowded round the fire, keeping their backs to it, and facing outward at the darkness of the forest. They went quickly to the caves and hurried back with branches and the fire pulsed out light with each addition. They began to bring whole skins of animals and wrap them round their bodies. The fat woman had ceased to wail for she was feeding the new one. Lok could see how the women stroked him fearfully, talked to him, offered him the shells from their necks and always looked outward to the dark ring of trees that trapped the firelight. Tuami and the old man were still talking urgently to each other with much nodding. Lok felt himself secure in the darkness but understood the impervious power of the people in the light. He called out:

"Where is Liku?"

He saw the people still their bodies and shrink. Only the child Tanakil began to scream until the crumpled woman seized her by the arm and shook her into silence.

"Give me Liku!"

Chestnut-head was listening sideways in the firelight, searching for the voice with his ear and his bent stick was rising.

"Where is Fa?"

The stick shrank and straightened suddenly. A moment later something brushed by in the air like the wing of a bird; there came a dry tap, then a wooden bounce and clatter. A woman rushed to the cave where Lok had crawled and brought a whole sheaf of branches and dumped them on the fire. The dark silhouettes of the people gazed into the forest inscrutably.

Lok turned away and trusted to his nose. He cast across the trail, found the scent of Fa and the scent of the two men who had followed her. He trotted forward, nose to the ground, along the scent that would bring him back to Fa. He had a great desire to hear her speak again and to touch her with his body. He moved faster through the darkness that preceded dawn and his nose told him, pace by pace, the whole story. Here were Fa's prints, far apart as she fled, the grip of her toes forcing back a little half-moon of earth out of the ground. He found that he could see more clearly now that he was away from the firelight for the dawn was breaking behind the trees. Once more the thought of Liku came to him. He turned back, swung himself into the cleft trunk of a beech tree and looked

through the branches at the clearing. The guard who had
run after Fa was dancing in front of the new people. He
crawled like a snake, he went to the wreck of the caves;
he stood; he came back to the fire snapping like a wolf so
that the people shrank from him. He pointed; he created
a running, crouching thing, his arms flapped like the
wings of a bird. He stopped by the thorn bushes,
sketched a line in the air over them, a line up and up towards the trees till it ended in a gesture of ignorance.
Tuami was talking rapidly to the old man. Lok saw him
kneel by the fire, clear a space and begin to draw on it
with a stick. There was no sign of Liku and the fat
woman was sitting in one of the hollow logs with the new
one on her shoulder.

Lok let himself down to the ground, found Fa's tracks
once more and ran along them. Her steps were full of
terror so that his own hair rose in sympathy. He came to
a place where the hunters had stopped and he could see
how one of them had stood sideways till his toeless feet
made deep marks in the earth. He saw the gap between
steps where Fa had leapt in the air and then her blood,
dropping thickly, leading in an uneven curve back from
the forest to the swamp where the tree-trunk had been.
He followed her into a tangle of briar that the hunters
had threshed over. He went in deeper than they, heedless
of the thorns that tore his skin. He saw where her feet
like his own had plunged terribly in the mud and left an
open hole that was filling now with stagnant water. Before him the surface of the marsh was polished and awe-
some. The bubbles had ceased to rise from the bottom
and any brown mud that had been whipped up to make
coils in the top water had sunk again as if nothing had

177

happened. Even the scum and the weed and clustering frog's spawn had drifted back and lay motionless in the dead water under the dirty boughs. The steps and the blood came thus far; there was the scent of Fa and her terror; and after that, nothing.

TEN

The drab light increased, silvered, and the black water of the marshes shone. A bird squawked among the islands of reed and briar. Far off, the stag of all stags blared and blared again. The mud round Lok's ankles tightened so that he had to balance with his arms. There was an astonishment in his head and beneath the astonishment a dull, heavy hunger that strangely included the heart. Automatically his nose inquired of the air for food and his eyes turned this way and that among the mud and tangles of briar. He lurched, bent his toes and drew his feet out of the mud and staggered to firmer land. The air was warm and tiny flying things sang thinly like the note that comes in the ears after a blow on the head. Lok shook himself but the high thin note continued and the heavy feeling weighed on his heart.

Where the trees began were bulbs with green points that just broke the ground. He turned these up with his feet, lifted them to his hand and put them to his mouth. Outside-Lok did not seem to want them, though inside-Lok made his teeth grind them and his throat rise and swallow. He remembered that he was thirsty and ran back to the marsh but the mud had changed; it was daunting now as it had not been before when he was following the scent of Fa. His feet would not enter it.

Lok began to bend. His knees touched the ground, his hands reached down and took his weight slowly, and with all his strength he clutched himself into the earth. He writhed himself against the dead leaves and twigs, his head came up, turned, and his eyes swept round, astonished eyes over a mouth that was strained open. The sound of mourning burst out of his mouth, prolonged, harsh, pain-sound, man-sound. The high note of the flying things continued and the fall droned at the foot of the mountain. Far off, the stag blared again.

There was pink in the sky and a new green in the tops of the trees. The buds that had been no more than points of life had opened into fingers so that their swarms had thickened against the light and only the larger branches were visible. The earth itself seemed to vibrate as though it were working to force the sap up the trunks. Slowly as the sounds of his mourning died away Lok attended to this vibration and was minutely comforted. He crawled, he took up bulbs with his fingers and chewed them, his throat rose and swallowed. He remembered his thirst again and went crouched and questing for firm ground by the water. He let himself head down from a raking branch, held with one hand and sucked at the dark onyx surface.

There was the sound of feet in the forest. He scrambled back to the firm earth and saw two of the new people flitting past the trunks with bent sticks in their hands. There were noises coming from the remainder of the people in the clearing; noises of logs moving over each other, and of trees being cut. He remembered Liku and ran away towards the clearing until he could peer over the bushes and see what the people were doing.

"A-ho! A-ho! A-ho!"

All at once he had a picture of the hollow logs nosing up the bank and coming to rest in the clearing. He crept forward and crouched. There were no more logs in the river, so no more would come out of it. He had another picture of the logs moving back into the river and this picture was so clearly connected in some way with the first one and the sounds from the clearing that he understood why one came out of the other. This was an upheaval in the brain and he felt proud and sad and like Mal. He spoke softly to the briars with their chains of new buds.

"Now I am Mal."

All at once it seemed to him that his head was new, as though a sheaf of pictures lay there to be sorted when he would. These pictures were of plain grey daylight. They showed the solitary string of life that bound him to Liku and the new one; they showed the new people towards whom both outside- and inside-Lok yearned with a terrified love, as creatures who would kill him if they could.

He had a picture of Liku looking up with soft and adoring eyes at Tanakil, guessed how Ha had gone with a kind of eager fearfulness to meet his sudden death. He clutched at the bushes as the tides of feeling swirled through him and howled at the top of his voice.

"Liku! Liku!"

The cutting noises stopped and became a long, grinding crackle instead. In front of him he saw Tuami's head and shoulders move quickly aside and then a whole tree with arms that bent and shattered in a mass of greenery came smashing down. As the green of the tree swept sideways he could see the clearing again for the thorn bushes had been torn down and the hollow logs were coming through. The people were heaving at the logs, inching them forward. Tuami was shouting and Bush was struggling to get his bent stick off his shoulder. Lok raced away until the people were small at the beginning of the trail.

The logs were not going back to the river but coming towards the mountain. He tried to see another picture that came out of this but could not; and then his head was Lok's head again and empty.

Tuami was hacking at the tree, not cutting the trunk itself but at the thin end where the arms stuck out, for Lok could hear the difference in the note. He could hear the old man too.

"A-ho! A-ho! A-ho!"

The log nosed along the trail. It rode on other logs, rollers that sank into the soft earth so that the people were gasping and crying out in their exhaustion and terror. The old man, though he did not touch the logs, was working harder than anybody. He ran round, commanded, exhorted, mimed their struggles, gasped with them; and his high bird-voice fluttered all the time. The women and Tanakil were ranged on either side of the hollow log and even the fat woman was heaving at the back. There was only one person in the log; the new one stood in the bottom, holding on to the side and gazing over at the uproarious commotion.

Tuami came back from the side of the trail dragging a great section of the tree-trunk. When he got it on to smooth ground he began to roll it towards the hollow log. The women gathered round the staring eyes, heaved up and forward and the log was rolling easily over the soft ground with the tree-trunk turning under it. The eyes dipped and Bush and Tuami came from behind with a smaller roller so that the log never touched the ground. There was a ceaseless movement and swirl like bees round a cleft in the rock, an ordered desperation. The log moved along the trail towards Lok with the new one swaying, bobbing up and down, mewing occasionally, but most of the time fastening his gaze on the nearest or most energetic of the people. As for Liku, she was nowhere to be seen; but Lok with a flash of Mal thinking remembered that there was another log and many bundles.

Just as the new one did nothing but look, so Lok was absorbed in their approach as a man who watches the tide come in may not remember to move until the spray washes at his feet. Only when they were so close to him that he could see how the grass flattened in front of the roller did he remember that the people were dangerous and flit away into the forest. He stopped when they were hidden from sight but still within earshot. The women were crying with the strain of pushing the log along and the old man was getting hoarse. Lok had so many feelings in his body that they bewildered him. He was frightened of the new people and sorry for them as for a woman who has the sickness. He began to roam about under the trees, picking at what food he could find but not minding if he did not find it. Pictures went from his head again and he became nothing but a vast well of feeling that could not be examined or denied. He thought at first he was hungry and crammed anything he could find into his mouth. Suddenly he found himself cramming in young branches, sour and useless inside their slippery bark. He was stuffing and gulping and then he was crouching on all fours, vomiting all the branches up again.

The noise of the people diminished a little until he could hear no more than the voice of the old man when it rose in command or fury. Down here where the forest changed to marsh and the sky opened over bushes, straggling willow and water, there was no other sign of their passage. The woodpigeons talked, preoccupied with their mating; nothing was changed, not even the great bough where a red-haired child had swung and laughed. All things profited and thrived in a warm windlessness. Lok got to his feet and wandered along by the marshes towards the mere where Fa had disappeared. To be Mal was proud and heavy. The new head knew that certain things were gone and done with like a wave of the sea. It knew that the misery must be embraced painfully as a man might hug thorns to him and it sought to comprehend the new people from whom all changes came.

Lok discovered "Like". He had used likeness all his life without being aware of it. Fungi on a tree were ears, the word was the same but acquired a distinction by circumstances that could never apply to the sensitive things on the side of his head. Now, in a convulsion of the understanding Lok found himself using likeness as a tool as surely as ever he had used a stone to hack at sticks or meat. Likeness could grasp the white-faced hunters with a hand, could put them into the world where they were thinkable and not a random and unrelated irruption.

He was picturing the hunters who went out with bent sticks in skill and malice.

"The people are like a famished wolf in the hollow of a tree."

He thought of the fat woman defending the new one from the old man, thought of her laughter, of men working at a single load and grinning at each other.

"The people are like honey trickling from a crevice in the rock."

He thought of Tanakil playing, her clever fingers, her laughter, and her stick.

"The people are like honey in the round stones, the new honey that smells of dead things and fire."

They had emptied the gap of its people with little more than a turn of their hands.

"They are like the river and the fall, they are a people of the fall; nothing stands against them."

He thought of their patience, of the broad man Tuami creating a stag out of coloured earth.

"They are like Oa."

There came a confusion in his head, a darkness; and then he was Lok again, wandering aimlessly by the marshes and the hunger that food would not satisfy was back. He could hear the people running along the trail to the clearing where the second log lay and they did not speak, but betrayed themselves by the thump and rustle of their steps. He shared a picture like a gleam of sunlight in winter that was gone before he had time to see it properly. He stopped, head up and nostrils flared. His ears took over the business of living, they discounted the noise of the people and concentrated on the moorhens that were driving their smooth breasts so furiously through the water. They came towards him in a wide angle, saw him and sheared off abruptly and all together to the right. A water rat followed them, nose up, body jerking inside the wave that it made. There was a washing sound, a swish and lap among the bushes of briar that dotted the marshes. Lok ran away then came back. He crouched through the mud and began to unlace the brambles that hid his view. The washing had stopped and the ripples from it were lapping the bushes, splashing into his footprints. He sought in the air with his nose, fought with the bushes and was through. He took three steps in the water and sank in mud crookedly. The washing began again and Lok, laughing and talking, took drunken steps towards it. The hair of outside-Lok rose at the touch of the cold stuff round his thighs and the grip of the unseen mud sucking at his feet. The heaviness, the hunger was rising, became a cloud that filled him, a cloud that the sun fills with fire. There was no heaviness any more but only the lightness that set him talking and laughing like the honey people, laughing and blinking water out of his eyes. Already they shared a picture.

"Here I am! I am coming!"

"Lok! Lok!"

Fa's arms were up, her fists doubled, her teeth clenched, she was leaning and forcing her way through the water. They were still covered to the thigh when they clung to each other and made clumsily for the bank. Before they could see their feet again in the squelching mud Lok was laughing and talking.

"It is bad to be alone. It is very bad to be alone."

Fa limped as she held him.

"I am hurt a little. The man did it with a stone on the end of a stick."

Lok touched the front of her thigh. The wound was no longer bleeding but black blood lay in it like a tongue.

"It is bad to be alone——"

"I ran into the water after the man hit me."

"The water is a terrible thing."

"The water is better than the new people."

Fa took her arm from his shoulder and they squatted down under a great beech. The people were returning from the clearing with the second hollow log. They were sobbing and gasping as they went. The two hunters who had gone off earlier were shouting down from the rocks of the mountain.

Fa stuck her wounded leg straight out in front of her.

"I ate eggs and reeds and the frog jelly."

Lok found that his hands kept reaching out and touching her. She smiled at him grimly. He remembered the instant connection that had made daylight of the disconnected pictures.

"Now I am Mal. It is heavy to be Mal."

"It is heavy to be the woman."

"The new people are like a wolf and honey, rotten honey and the river."

"They are like a fire in the forest."

Quite suddenly Lok had a picture from so deep down in his head he had not known it was there. For a moment the picture seemed to be outside him so that the world changed. He himself was the same size as before but everything else had grown suddenly bigger. The trees were mountainous. He was not on the ground but riding on a back and he was holding to reddish-brown hair with hands and feet. The head in front of him, though he could not see the face was Mal's face and a greater Fa fled ahead of him. The trees above were flailing up flames and the breath from them was attacking him. There was urgency and that same tightening of the skin—there was terror.

"Now is like when the fire flew away and ate up the trees."

The sounds of the people and their logs were far in the distance. Runners came thumping back along the trail to the clearing. There came a moment of bird-speech, then silence. The steps thumped back along the trail and faded again. Fa and Lok stood up and went towards the trail. They did not speak but in their cautious, circling approach was the unspoken admission that the people could not be left alone. Terrible they might be as the fire or the river but they drew like honey or meat. The trail had changed like everything else that the people had touched. The earth was gouged and scattered, the rollers had depressed and smoothed a way broad enough for Lok and Fa and another to walk abreast.

"They pushed their hollow logs on trees that rolled along. The new one was in a log. And Liku will be in the other."

Fa looked mournfully at his face. She pointed to a smear on the smoothed earth that had been a slug.

"They have gone over us like a hollow log. They are like a winter."

The feeling was back in Lok's body; but with Fa standing before him it was a heaviness that could be borne.

"Now there are only Fa and Lok and the new one and Liku."

For a while she looked at him in silence. She put out a hand and he took it. She opened her mouth to speak but no sound came. She gave a shake of her whole body and then started to shudder. He could see her master this shudder as if she were leaving the comfort of the cave in a morning of snow. She took her hand away.

"Come!"

The fire was still smouldering in a great ring of ash. The shelters were torn apart though the uprights still stood. As for the ground in the clearing it had been churned up as though a whole herd of cattle had stampeded there. Lok crept to the edge of the clearing while Fa hung back. He began to circle. In the centre of the clearing were the pictures and the gifts.

When Fa saw these she moved inward behind Lok, and they approached them spirally, ears cocked for the return of the new people. The pictures were confused by the fire where the stag's head still watched Lok inscrutably. There was a new stag now, spring-coloured and fat, but another figure lay across it. This figure was red, with enormous spreading arms and legs and the face glared up at him for the eyes were white pebbles. The hair stood out round the head as though the figure were in the act of some frantic cruelty, and through the figure, pinning it to the stag, was a stake driven deep, its end split and furred over. The two people retreated from it in awe, for they had never seen any thing like it. Then they returned timidly to the presents.

The whole haunch of a stag, raw but comparatively bloodless, hung from the top of the stake and an opened stone of honey-drink stood by the staring head. The

189

scent of the honey rose out of it like the smoke and flame from a fire. Fa put out her hand and touched the meat which swung so that she snatched her hand back. Lok fetched another circle round the figure, his feet avoiding the outstretched limbs while his hand moved out slowly. In a moment they were tearing at the present, ripping apart the muscle and cramming the raw meat into their mouths. They did not stop till they were skin tight with food and a shining white bone hung from the stake by a strip of hide.

At last Lok stood back and wiped his hands on his thighs. Still with nothing said they turned in towards each other and squatted by the pot. From far off on the slope leading to the terrace they could hear the old man.

"A-ho! A-ho! A-ho!"

The reek from the open mouth of the pot was thick. A fly meditated on the lip, then as Lok's breathing came closer, shuffled its wings, flew for a moment and landed again.

Fa put her hand on Lok's wrist.

"Do not touch it."

But Lok's mouth was close to the pot, his nostrils wide, his breathing quick. He spoke in a loud cracked voice.

"Honey."

All at once he ducked, thrust his mouth into the pot and sucked. The rotten honey burnt his mouth and tongue so that he somersaulted backwards and Fa fled from the pot round the ashes of the fire. She stood looking fearfully at him while he spat and began to crawl back stalking the pot that waited for him, reeking. He lowered himself cautiously and sipped. He smacked his lips and sucked again. He sat back and laughed in her face.

"Drink."

Uncertainly she bent to the mouth of the pot and put her tongue in the stinging, sweet stuff. Lok suddenly knelt forward, talking, and pushed her away so that she was astonished and squatted, licking her lips and spitting. Lok burrowed into the pot and sucked three times; but at the third suck the surface of the honey slid out of reach so that he sucked air and choked explosively. He rolled on the ground, trying to get back his breath. Fa tried for the honey but could not reach it with her tongue and spoke bitterly to him. She stood silent for a moment then picked up the pot and held it to her mouth as the new people did. Lok saw her with the great stone at her face and laughed and tried to tell her how funny she was. He remembered the honey in time, leapt up and tried to take the stone from her face. But it was stuck, glued, and as he dragged it down her face came with it. Then they were pulling and shouting at each other. Lok heard his voice coming out, high and loud and savage. He let go to examine this new voice and Fa staggered away with the pot. He found that the trees were moving very gently sideways and upwards. He had a magnificent picture that would put everything right and tried to describe it to Fa who would not listen. Then he had nothing but the picture of having had a picture and this made him furiously angry. He reached out after the picture with his voice and he heard it, disconnected from inside-Lok, laughing and quacking like a duck. But there was one word that was the beginning of the picture even though the picture itself had gone out of sight. He held on to the word. He stopped laughing and spoke very solemnly to Fa who was still standing with the stone at her face.

"Log!" he said. "Log!"

Then he remembered the honey and indignantly pulled the stone from her. Immediately her red face came out of the pot she started to laugh and talk. Lok held the pot as the new people had held it and the honey flowed over his chest. He writhed his body until his face was under the pot and contrived to get the trickle into his mouth. Fa was shrieking with laughter. She fell over, rolled, and lay back kicking her legs in the air. Lok and the honey fire responded to this invitation clumsily. Then they both remembered the pot and were pulling and arguing once more. Fa managed to drink a little but the honey turned sulky and would not come out. Lok snatched the pot, wrestled with it, beat it with his fist, shouted; but there was no more honey. He hurled the pot at the ground in fury and it grinned open into two pieces. Lok and Fa flung themselves at the pieces, squatted, each licking and turning a piece over to find where the honey had gone. The fall was roaring in the clearing, inside Lok's head. The trees were moving faster. He sprang to his feet and found that the ground was as perilous as a log. He struck at a tree as it came past to keep it still and then he was lying on his back with the sky spinning over him. He turned over, and got up rump first, swaying like the new one. Fa was crawling round the ashes of the fire like a moth with a burnt wing. She was talking to herself about hyenas. All at once Lok discovered the power of the new people in him. He was one of them, there was nothing he could not do. There were many branches left in the clearing and unburnt logs. Lok ran sideways to a log and commanded it to move. He shouted.

"A-ho! A-ho! A-ho!"

The log was sliding like the trees but not fast enough.

He went on shouting but the log would not move any faster. He seized a branch and struck again and again at the log as Tanakil had struck at Liku. He had a picture of people on either side of the log, straining, mouths open. He shouted at them like the old man

Fa was crawling past. She was moving slowly, deliberately as the log and the trees. Lok swung the stick at her rump with a great yell and the splintered end of the branch flew off and bounded among the trees. Fa screeched and staggered to her feet so that Lok struck again and missed. She swung round and they were standing face to face, shouting and the trees were sliding. He saw her right breast move, her arm come up, her open palm in the air, a palm somehow of importance that any moment now would become a thing he must attend to. Then the side of his face was struck by lightning that dazzled the world and the earth stood up and hit his right side a thunderous blow. He leaned against this vertical ground while the side of his face opened and shut and flames burst out of it. Fa was lying down, receding and coming close. Then she was pulling him up or down, there was solid earth under his feet again and he was hanging on to her. They were weeping and laughing at each other and the fall was roaring in the clearing while the shock head of the dead tree was climbing away into the sky, only getting larger instead of smaller. He became frightened in a detached way, he knew it would be good to get close to her. He put aside the strangeness and sleepiness of his head; he peered for her, bored at her face which kept receding like the shock-headed tree. The trees were still sliding but steadily as though it had always been their nature to do so.

He spoke to her through the mists.

"I am one of the new people."

This made him caper. Then he walked through the clearing with what he thought was the slow swaying carriage of the new people. The picture came to him that Fa must cut off his finger. He lumbered round the clearing, trying to find her and tell her so. He found her behind the tree near the edge of the river and she was being sick. He told her about the old woman in the water but she took no notice so he went back to the broken pot and licked the traces of decaying honey off it. The figure on the ground became the old man and Lok told him that there was now an addition to the new people. Then he felt very tired so that the ground became soft and the pictures in his head went round and round. He explained to the man that now Lok must go back to the overhang but that reminded him even with his spinning head that there was no overhang any more. He began to mourn, loudly and easily and the mourning was very pleasant. He found that when he looked at the trees they slid apart and could only be induced to come together with a great effort that he was not disposed to make. All at once there was nothing but sunlight and the voice of the woodpigeons over the drone of the fall. He lay back, his eyes open, watching the strange pattern that the doubled branches made against the sky. His eyes closed themselves and he fell down as over a cliff of sleep.

ELEVEN

Fa was shaking him.

"They are going away."

Hands not Fa's hands were gripped round his head, producing a hot pain. He groaned and rolled away from the hands but they held on, squeezing until the pain was inside his head.

"The new people are going away. They are taking their hollow logs up the slope to the terrace."

Lok opened his eyes and yelped with pain for he seemed to be looking straight into the sun. Water ran out of his eyes and blazed fiercely between the lids. Fa shook him again. He felt for the ground with his hands and feet and lifted himself a little way from it. His stomach contracted and all at once he was sick. His stomach had a life of its own; it rose in a hard knot, would have nothing to do with this evil, honey-smelling stuff and rejected it. Fa was taking by his shoulder.

"My stomach has been sick too."

He turned over again, and squatted laboriously without opening his eyes. He could feel the sunlight burning down one side of his face.

"They are going away. We must take back the new one."

Lok prised open his eyes, looked out cautiously between gummed-up lids to see what had happened to the world. It was brighter. The earth and the trees were made of nothing but colour and swayed so that he shut his eyes again.

"I am ill."

For a while she said nothing. Lok discovered that the hands holding his head were inside it and they squeezed so tightly that he could feel blood pulsing through his brain. He opened his eyes, blinked, and the world settled a little. There were still the blazing colours but they were not swaying. In front of him the earth was rich brown and red, the trees were silver and green and the branches were covered with spurts of green fire. He squatted, blinking, feeling the tenderness of his face while Fa went on speaking.

"I was sick and you would not wake up. I went to see the new people. Their hollow logs have moved up the slope. The new people are frightened. They stand and move like people who are frightened. They heave and sweat and watch the forest over their backs. But there is no danger in the forest. They are frightened of the air where there is nothing. Now we must get the new one from them."

Lok put his hands to the earth on either side of him. The sky was bright and the world blazed with colour, but it was still the world he knew.

"We must take Liku from them."

Fa stood up and ran round the clearing. She came back and looked down at him. He got up carefully.

"Fa says 'Do this!' "

He waited obediently. Mal had gone out of his head.

"Here is a picture. Lok goes up the path by the cliff where the people cannot see him. Fa goes round and climbs to the mountain above the people. They will follow. The men will follow. Then Lok takes the new one from the fat woman and runs."

She took hold of him by the arms and looked imploringly into his face.

"There will be a fire again. And I shall have children."

A picture came into Lok's head.

"I will do so," he said sturdily, "and when I see Liku I will take her also."

There were things in Fa's face, not for the first time, that he could not understand.

They parted at the foot of the slope where the bushes still hid them from the new people. Lok went to the right and Fa flitted away along the skirts of the forest to make a great circle round the slope. When Lok glanced back he could see her, red as a squirrel, running mostly on all fours in the cover of the trees. He began to climb, listening for voices. He came out on the track above the water, with the fall roaring ahead of him. There was more water coming over than ever. There was a profounder thunder from the basin at the foot and the smoke was spread far over the island. The sheets of falling water shook out into milky skeins, unspun into a creamy substance that was hard to distinguish from the leaping spray and mist that rose to meet it. Beyond the island he could see great trees in all their spring foliage sliding over the lip. They would vanish into the spray and then appear again beyond it, shattered and leaning in the water of the river, jerking as if a gigantic hand were plucking at them beneath. But on this side of the island no trees came over; only a ceaseless abundance of shining water and creamy milk falling into noise and white, drifting smoke.

Then, through all the noise of the water he heard the voices of the new people. They were on the right, hidden by the rising rock where the ice woman had hung. He paused and heard them screaming at each other.

Here, with the so familiar sights about him, with the history of his people still hanging round the rocks, his misery returned with a new strength. The honey had not killed the misery but put it to sleep for a while so that now it was refreshed. He groaned at emptiness and had a great feeling for Fa on the other side of the slope. There was Liku too somewhere among the people and his need of either or both became urgent. He set himself to climb up the crack where the ice woman had hung and the sounds of the new people were louder. Presently he was lying at the lip of the cliff, looking over a hand's breadth of earth and straggling grass and stunted bushes.

Once more the new people were performing for him. They had done meaningless things with logs. Some were wedged in rocks with others lying across them. The scarred earth of the slope led right on to the terrace so that he understood that the other log had reached the overhang. The one the people were working at now was pointing up the slope between the wedged logs. There were strips of thick and twisted hide leading from it. There was a log wedged crosswise behind the hollow log, balanced at its mid-point against an outcrop and this nearer end was bending with the weight of a boulder that wanted to roll downhill. As Lok caught sight of it, he saw the old man pull a strip of twisted hide and the boulder was free. It pushed against the log, forcing it down the slope and the hollow log slid in the other direction towards the terrace. The boulder did all its work and went bumping away down to the forest. Tuami had jammed a stone behind the hollow log and the people were shouting. There were no more boulders between the log and the terrace so that now the people did the boulder's work. They laid hold of the log and heaved. The old man stood by them and a dead snake hung from his right hand. He began to cry—a-ho! and the people strained till their faces crumpled. The old man raised the snake in the air and struck with it at the shuddering backs. The log moved onwards.

After a while Lok noticed the other people. The fat woman was not pushing. She was standing well to one side between Lok and the hollow log and she was holding the new one. Now Lok could see what Fa meant by the fright of the new people, for the fat woman was glancing round all the time and her face was even paler than it had been in the clearing. Tanakil stood close by her so that she was partly hidden. As if his eyes had been opened Lok could see how the frantic heaving at the log was made strong by this fear. The people consented to the dead snake if it would call from their bodies, already so thin, the strength they could not command themselves. There was a hysterical speed in the efforts of Tuami and in the screaming voice of the old man. They were retreating up the slope as though cats with their evil teeth were after them, as though the river itself were flowing uphill. Yet the river stayed in its bed and the slope was bare of all but the new people.

"They are frightened óf the air."

Pine-tree yelled and slipped and instantly Tuami had

the rock jammed against the back of the log. The people gathered round Pine-tree, babbling, and the old man flourished his snake. Tuami was pointing up the mountainside. He ducked and a stone struck the hollow log with a thump. The babble became a shriek. Tuami, leaning with all his strength, was holding the log on a single length of hide while it ground sideways. He fastened the hide to a rock and then the men spread out in a line facing the mountain. Fa was visible, a small red figure dancing on the rock above them. Lok saw her swing her arm and another stone came humming through the line. The men were bending their sticks and letting them straighten suddenly. Lok saw twigs fly up the rock, falter before they reached Fa, turn and come back again. Another stone broke on the rock by the log and the fat woman came running to the cliff where Lok was. She stopped and turned back but Tanakil came on, right to the lip. She saw him and screeched. He was up, had grabbed her before the fat woman had time to turn again. He seized Tanakil by her thin arms and talked to her urgently.

"Where is Liku! Tell me, where is Liku?"

At the sound of Liku's name Tanakil began to struggle and scream as though she had fallen into deep water. The fat woman was screaming too and the new one had scrambled to her shoulder. The old man was running along the lip of the cliff. Chestnut-head was coming from where the log was. He rushed straight at Lok and his teeth were bare. The screaming and the teeth terrified Lok. He let Tanakil go so that she reeled back. Her foot struck Chestnut-head's knee just as he launched himself at Lok. He travelled through the air past Lok, grunting faintly and went over the cliff. He just fitted the delicate curve of the descent so that he seemed to skim down on his belly, never more than a hand's breadth away from rock but never touching it. He vanished and did not even leave a scream behind him. The old man flung a stick at Lok who could see that there was a sharp stone on the end and avoided it. Then he was running between the fat woman with her mouth open and Tanakil flat on her back. The men who had thrown twigs at Fa had turned and were watching Lok. He went very fast across the slope until he reached the strip of hide that held the log. He ran through this and it took most of the skin off his shin before it gave. The log began to slide backwards. The people ceased to watch Lok and watched the log instead so that he turned his head as he ran to see what they were looking at. The log got up speed on two rollers but after that they were not necessary. It left the slope where the descent steepened and travelled on through the air. The back end hit a point of rock and the log opened in two halves all along its length. The two halves went on, turning round and round until they smashed into the forest. Lok leapt into a gully and the people were out of sight.

Fa was jumping about at the head of the gully and he ran towards her as fast as he could. The men were advancing across the rocks with their bent sticks but he reached her first. They were about to climb further when the men stopped for the old man was shouting at them. Even without knowing the words Lok could understand his gestures. The men ran down the rock and were lost to view.

Fa was showing her teeth too.

She came at Lok brandishing her arms and there was still a sharp stone in one hand.

"Why did you not snatch the new one?"

Lok put out his hands defensively.

"I asked for Liku. I asked Tanakil."

Fa's arms came down slowly.

"Come!"

The sun was sinking towards the gap and making a whirl of gold and red. They could see the new people hurrying about on the terrace as Fa led the way towards the cliff above the overhang. The new people had shifted the hollow log to the upriver end of the terrace and were trying to get it past the jam of tree-trunks that now lay where Lok and Fa had crossed to the island. They slid it from the terrace and it lay in the water with logs all round it. The men were heaving at the tree-trunks, trying to deflect them to the other side of the rock where they would be swept away over the fall. Fa ran about on the mountainside.

"They will take the new one with them."

She began to run down the steep rock as the sun sank into the gap. There was red now over the mountains and the ice women were on fire. Lok shouted suddenly and Fa stopped and looked down at the water. There was a tree coming towards the jam; not a small trunk or a splintered fragment but a whole tree from some forest over the horizon. It was coming along this side of the gap, a colony of budding twigs and branches, a vast, half-hidden trunk, and roots that spread above the water and held enough earth between them to make a hearth for all the people in the world. As it came into sight the old man began to yell and dance. The women looked up from the bundles they were lowering into the hollow log and the men scrambled back across the jam. The roots struck the jam and splintered logs leapt into the air or stood up slowly. They caught the roots and hung. The tree stopped moving and swung sideways until it lay along the cliff beyond the terrace. Now there was a tangle of logs between the hollow log and the open water like a huge line of thorns. The jam had become an impassable barrier.

The old man stopped shouting. He ran to one of the bundles and began to open it. He shouted to Tuami who ran, holding Tanakil by the hand. They were coming along the terrace.

"Quickly!"

Fa fled away down the side of the mountain towards the entrance to the terrace and the overhang. As she ran she shouted to Lok:

"We will take Tanakil. Then they will give back the new one."

The rock was different. The colours that had drenched the world when Lok awoke from his honey sleep were richer, deeper. He seemed to leap and scamper through a tide of red air and the shadows behind the rocks were mauve. He dropped down the slope.

Together they stopped at the entrance to the terrace and crouched. The river was running crimson and there were golden flashes on it. The mountains on the other side of the river had become so dark that Lok had to peer at it before he discovered that it was dark blue. The jam and the tree and the toiling figures on it were black. But the terrace and the overhang were still brightly lit by the

203

red light. The stag was dancing again, dancing on the slope of earth that led up to the overhang and he faced into the space where Mal had died before the right-hand recess. He was black against the fire where the sun was sinking and as he moved he wielded long rays of sunlight that dazzled the eyes. Tuami was working in the overhang, smearing colour on a shape that stood between the two recesses against the pillar. Tanakil was there, a small, thin, black figure crouching where the fire had been.

From the other end of the terrace came a rhythmic clop! clop! Two of the men were cutting at the log that Lok had jammed. The sun buried itself in cloud, red shot up to the top of the sky and the mountains were black.

The stag blared. Tuami came running out of the overhang, running towards the jam where the men were working and Tanakil started to scream. The clouds swarmed over the sun and the pressure went out of the redness so that it seemed to float in the gap like a thinner water. Now the stag was bounding away towards the jam and the men were struggling with the log like beetles on a dead bird.

Lok ran forward and Tanakil's scream echoed the screams of Liku crossing the water so that they frightened him. He stood in the entrance to the overhang, gibbering.

"Where is Liku? What have you done with Liku?"

Tanakil's body straightened, arched, and her eyes rolled. She stopped screaming and lay on her back and there was blood between her grinning teeth. Fa and Lok crouched in front of her.

The overhang had altered like everything else. Tuami had made a figure for the old man and it stood there against the pillar and glared at them. They could see how quickly, savagely he had worked for the figure was smeared and not filled in as carefully as the figures in the clearing. It was some kind of man. Its arms and legs were contracted as though it were leaping forward and it was red as the water had been. There was hair standing out on all sides of the head as the hair of the old man had stood out when he was enraged or frightened. The face was a daub of clay but the pebbles were there, staring blindly. The old man had taken the teeth from his neck and stuck them in the face and finished them off with the two great cat's teeth from his ears. There was a stick driven into a crack in the creature's breast and to this stick was fastened a strip of hide; and to the other end of the hide was fastened Tanakil.

Fa began to make noises. They were not words and they were not screams. She seized the stick and began to heave but it would not come for the end was furred where Tuami had driven it in. Lok pushed her to one side and pulled but the stick stayed where it was. The red light was lifting from the water and the overhang was full of shadow through which the creature glared with eyes and teeth.

"Pull!"

He swung all his weight on the stick and felt it bend. He lifted his feet, planted them in the figure's red belly and thrust until his muscles ached. The mountain seemed to move and the figure slid so that its arms were about to grasp him. Then the stick whipped out of the crack and he was rolling with it on the ground.

"Bring her quickly."

Lok staggered to his feet, picked up Tanakil and ran

after Fa along the terrace. There came a screaming from the figures by the hollow log and a loud bang from the jam. The tree began to move forward and the logs were lumbering about like the legs of a giant. The crumple-faced woman was struggling with Tuami on the rock by the hollow log; she burst free and came running towards Lok. There was movement everywhere, screaming, demoniac activity; the old man was coming across the tumbling logs. He threw something at Fa. Hunters were holding the hollow log against the terrace and the head of the tree with all its weight of branches and wet leaves was drawing along them. The fat woman was lying in the log, the crumpled woman was in it with Tanakil, the old man was tumbling into the back. The boughs crashed and drew along the rock with an agonized squealing. Fa was sitting by the water holding her head. The branches took her. She was moving with them out into the water and the hollow log was free of the rock and drawing away. The tree swung into the current with Fa sitting limply among the branches. Lok began to gibber again. He ran up and down on the terrace. The tree would not be cajoled or persuaded. It moved to the edge of the fall, it swung until it was lying along the lip. The water reared up over the trunk, pushing, the roots were over. The tree hung for a while with the head facing upstream. Slowly the root end sank and the head rose. Then it slid forward soundlessly and dropped over the fall.

The red creature stood on the edge of the terrace and did nothing. The hollow log was a dark spot on the water towards the place where the sun had gone down. The air in the gap was clear and blue and calm. There was no

noise at all now except for the fall, for there was no wind
and the green sky was clear. The red creature turned to
the right and trotted slowly towards the far end of the
terrace. Water was cascading down the rocks beyond the
terrace from the melting ice in the mountains. The river
was high and flat and drowned the edge of the terrace.
There were long scars in the earth and rock where the
branches of a tree had been dragged past by the water.
The red creature came trotting back to a dark hollow in
the side of the cliff where there was evidence of occupa-
tion. It looked at the other figure, dark now, that grinned
down at it from the back of the hollow. Then it turned
away and ran through the little passage that joined the
terrace to the slope. It halted, peering down at the scars,
the abandoned rollers and broken ropes. It turned again,
sidled round a shoulder of rock and stood on an almost
imperceptible path that ran along the sheer rocks. It
began to sidle along the path, crouched, its long arms
swinging, touching, almost as firm a support as the legs.
It was peering down into the thunderous waters but
there was nothing to be seen but the columns of glimmering haze where the water had scooped a bowl out of
the rock. It moved faster, broke into a queer loping run
that made the head bob up and down and the forearms
alternate like the legs of a horse. It stopped at the end of
the path and looked down at the long streamers of weed
that were moving backwards and forwards under the
water. It put up a hand and scratched under its chinless
mouth. There was a tree, far away in the gleaming reaches
of the river, a tree in leaf that was rolling over and over
as the current thrust it towards the sea. The red creature,
now grey and blue in the twilight, loped down the slope

and dived into the forest. It followed a track broad and scarred as a cart-track, until it came to a clearing by the river beneath a dead tree. It scrambled about by the water, clambered up the tree, peered through the ivy after the tree in the river. Then it came down, raced along a trail that led through the bushes by the river until it came to an arm that broke the trail. Here it paused, then ran to and fro by the water. It seized a great swinging beech bough and lugged it back and forwards until its breathing was fierce and uneven. It ran back to the clearing, began to circle round and between the thorn bushes that had been laid there in heaps. It made no sound. There were stars pricking out and the sky was no longer green, but dark blue. A white owl floated through the clearing to its nest among the trees of the island on the other side of the river. The creature paused and looked down at some smears by what had been a fire.

Now that the sunlight had gone completely, no longer even throwing light into the sky from below the horizon, the moon took over. Shadows began to sharpen, leading from every tree and tangling behind the bushes. The red creature began to sniff round by the fire. Its weight was on its knuckles and it worked with its nose lowered almost to the ground. A water rat returning to the river glimpsed the four legs and flashed sideways under a bush to lie there waiting. The creature stopped between the ashes of the fire and the forest. It shut its eyes, and breathed in quickly. It began to scramble in the earth, its nose always searching. Out of the churned-up earth the right forepaw picked a small, white bone.

It straightened up a little and stood, not looking at the bone but at a spot some distance ahead. It was a strange creature, smallish, and bowed. The legs and thighs were bent and there was a whole thatch of curls on the outside of the legs and the arms. The back was high, and covered over the shoulders with curly hair. Its feet and hands were broad, and flat, the great toe projecting inwards to grip. The square hands swung down to the knees. The head was set slightly forward on the strong neck that seemed to lead straight on to the row of curls under the lip. The mouth was wide and soft and above the curls of the upper lip the great nostrils were flared like wings. There was no bridge to the nose and the moon-shadow of the jutting brow lay just above the tip. The shadows lay most darkly in the caverns above its cheeks and the eyes were invisible in them. Above this again, the brow was a straight line fledged with hair; and above that there was nothing.

The creature stood and the splashes of moonlight stirred over it. The eye-hollows gazed not at the bone but at an invisible point towards the river. Now the right leg began to move. The creature's attention seemed to gather and focus in the leg and the foot began to pick and search in the earth like a hand. The big toe bored and gripped and the toes folded round an object that had been almost completely buried in the churned soil. The foot rose, the leg bent and presented an object to the lowered hand. The head came down a little, the gaze swept inward from that invisible point and regarded what was in the hand. It was a root, old and rotted, worn away at both ends but preserving the exaggerated contours of a female body.

The creature looked again towards the water. Both hands were full, the bar of its brow glistened in the moonlight, over the great caverns where the eyes were hidden.

There was light poured down over the cheek-bones and the wide lips and there was a twist of light caught like a white hair in every curl. But the caverns were dark as though already the whole head was nothing but a skull.

The water rat concluded from the creature's stillness that it was not dangerous. It came with a quick rush from under the bush and began to cross the open space, it forgot the silent figure and searched busily for something to eat.

There was light now in each cavern, lights faint as the starlight reflected in the crystals of a granite cliff. The lights increased, acquired definition, brightened, lay each sparkling at the lower edge of a cavern. Suddenly, noiselessly, the lights became thin crescents, went out, and streaks glistened on each cheek. The lights appeared again, caught among the silvered curls of the beard. They hung, elongated, dropped from curl to curl and gathered at the lowest tip. The streaks on the cheeks pulsed as the drops swam down them, a great drop swelled at the end of a hair of the beard, shivering and bright. It detached itself and fell in a silver flash, striking a withered leaf with a sharp pat. The water rat scurried away and plopped into the river.

Stealthily the moonlight moved the blue shadows. The creature pulled its right foot out of the mire and took a lurching step forward. It staggered in a half-circle until it reached the gap between the thorn bushes where the broad track began. It started to run along the track and it was blue and grey in the moonlight. It went laboriously, slowly, with much bobbing up and down of the head. It limped. When it reached the slope up to the top of the fall it was on all fours.

On the terrace the creature moved faster. It ran to the far end where the water was coming down from the ice in a cascade. It turned, came back, and crept on all fours into the hollow where the other figure was. The creature wrestled with a rock that was lying on a mound of earth but was too weak to move it. At last it gave up and crawled round the hollow by the remains of a fire. It came close to the ashes and lay on its side. It pulled its legs up, knees against the chest. It folded its hands under its cheek and lay still. The twisted and smoothed root lay before its face. It made no noise, but seemed to be growing into the earth, drawing the soft flesh of its body into a contact so close that the movements of pulse and breathing were inhibited.

There were eyes like green fires above the hollow and grey dogs that slid and sidled through the moon-shadows. They descended to the terrace and approached the overhang. They sniffed curiously and cautiously at the earth outside the hollow but did not dare to approach nearer. Slowly the procession of stars sank behind the mountain and the night waned. There was grey light on the terrace and a little wind of dawn, blowing through the gap in the mountains. The ashes stirred, lifted, turned over and scattered themselves across the motionless body. The hyenas sat, tongues lolling, panting rapidly.

The sky over the sea turned to pink and then to gold. Light and colour came back. They showed the two red shapes, the one glaring from the rock the other, moulded into the earth, sandy, and chestnut and red. The water from the ice increased in volume, sparkling out into the gap in a long curved fall. The hyenas lifted their hind-quarters off the earth, separated and approached the interior of the hollow from either hand. The ice crowns of the mountains were a-glitter. They welcomed the sun. There was a sudden tremendous noise that set the hyenas shivering back to the cliff. It was a noise that engulfed the water noises, rolled along the mountains, boomed from cliff to cliff and spread in a tangle of vibrations over the sunny forests and out towards the sea.

TWELVE

Tuami sat in the stern of the dug-out, the steering paddle under his left arm. There was plenty of light and the patches of salt no longer looked like holes in the skin sail. He thought bitterly of the great square sail they had left bundled up in that last mad hour among the mountains; for with that and the breeze through the gap he need not have endured these hours of strain. He need not have sat all night wondering whether the current would beat the wind and bear them back to the fall while the people or as many as were left of them slept their collapsed sleep. Still, they had moved on, the walls of rock folding back until this lake became so broad that he had been able to find no transits for judging their motion but had sat, guessing, with the mountains looming over the flat water and his eyes red with the tears of strain. Now he stirred a little for the rounded bilge was hard and the pad of leather that many steersmen had moulded to a comfortable seat was lost on the slope up from the forest. He could feel the slight pressure transmitted to his forearm along the loom of the paddle and knew that if he were to trail his hand over the side the water would tinkle against the palm and heap up over his wrist. The two dark lines spreading on either bow were not laid back at a sharp angle but led out almost at right angles to the line of the boat. If the breeze changed or faltered those lines would creep ahead and fade and the pressure in the paddle would slacken and they would begin to slide astern towards the mountains.

He shut his eyes and passed a hand wearily over his forehead. The breeze might die away and then they would be forced to paddle with what strength the journey had left them in order to reach a shore before the current bore them back. He jerked his hand away and glanced at the sail. It was full but pulsing gently, the double sheets that led aft here to the belaying pins were moving together, moving apart, moving up and down. He looked away at the miles of now visible grey water and there was a monster sliding past, not half a cable to starboard, the root lifted above the surface like a mammoth's tusk. It was sliding towards the fall and the forest devils. The dug-out was hanging still, waiting for the wind to die away. He tried to perform a calculation in his aching head, tried to balance the current, the wind, the dug-out but he could come to no conclusion.

He shook himself irritably and parallel lines rippled out from the sides of the boat. A fair wind, steerage-way, and plenty of water all round—what more could a man want? Those hardening clouds on either hand were hills with trees on them. Forrard there under the sail was what looked like lower land, plains perhaps where men could hunt in the open, not stumble among dark trees or on hard, haunted rocks. What more could a man want?

But this was confusion. He rested his eyes on the back of his left hand and tried to think. He had hoped for the light as for a return to sanity and the manhood that seemed to have left them; but here was dawn—past dawn —and they were what they had been in the gap, haunted, bedevilled, full of strange irrational grief like himself, or emptied, collapsed, and helplessly asleep. It seemed as though the portage of the boats—or boat rather, now she was gone—from that forest to the top of the fall had taken them on to a new level not only of land but of experience and emotion. The world with the boat moving so slowly at the centre was dark amid the light, was untidy, hopeless, dirty.

He waggled the paddle in the water and the sheets tossed. The sail made a sleepy remark and then was attentively full again. Perhaps if they squared off the boat, stowed things properly——? Partly to assess the job and partly to turn his eyes outwards from his own mind, Tuami examined the hollow hull before him.

The bundles lay where the women had thrown them. Those two on the port side amidships made a tent for Vivani though with her usual contrariness she preferred a shelter of leaves and branches. There was a bundle of spears under them and they were being spoiled because Bata was sleeping on them face down. He would find the shafts bent or cracked and the good flint-points broken. To starboard was a jumble of skins that was of little use to anyone, but the women had thrown it in when they might have kept the sail instead. One of the empty pots was broken and the other lay on its side with the clay plug still in place. There would be little to drink but water. Vivani lay curled on the useless skins—had she made them place the skins there for comfort, not bothering with the precious sail? It would be like her. She was covered with a magnificent skin, the cave-bear skin that had cost two lives to get and was the price her first man paid for her. What was a sail, thought Tuami bitterly, when Vivani wanted to be comfortable? What a fool Marlan was, at his age, to have run off with her for her great heart and wit, her laughter and her white, incredible body! And what fools we were to come with him, forced by his magic, or at any rate forced by some compulsion there are no words for! He looked at Marlan, hating him, and thought of the ivory dagger that he had been grinding so slowly to a point. Marlan sat facing aft, his legs stretched in the bottom, his head resting against the mast. His mouth was open and his hair and beard were like a grey bush. Tuami could see in the growing light how strength had gone out of him. There had been lines before round the mouth, deep channels from the nostrils downwards but now the face behind the hair was not only lined but thin. There was utter exhaustion in the slanted fall of the head and in the jaw pulled down and sideways. Not long now, thought Tuami, when we are safe and out of the devil's country I shall dare to use the ivory-point.

Even so to watch Marlan's face and intend to kill him was daunting. He turned his eyes away, glimpsed the huddle of bodies in the bow beyond the mast and then looked down past his own feet. Tanakil lay there, flat on her back. She was not drained of life like Marlan but rather had life in abundance, a new life, not her own. She did not move much and her quick breathing fluttered a scrap of dried blood that hung on her lower lip. The eyes were neither asleep nor awake. Now he could see them clearly he saw that the night was going on in them for they were sunken and dark, opaquenesses without intelligence. Though he leaned forward where she must have seen him her eyes did not focus on his face but continued to strain inward towards the night. Twal, who lay by her, had one arm stretched protectively across her. Twal's body looked like the body of an old woman, though she was younger than he and was Tanakil's mother.

Tuami rubbed a hand across his forehead again. If I could drop this paddle and work at my dagger or if I had charcoal and a flat stone—he looked desperately round the boat for something on which to fasten his attention— I am like a pool, he thought, some tide has filled me, the sand is swirling, the waters are obscured and strange things are creeping out of the cracks and crannies in my mind.

The skin at Vivani's feet stirred, lifted and he thought she was waking up. Then a small leg, red, covered with curls and no longer than his hand stretched itself in the air. It felt round, tried the surface of the pot and rejected it, touched skin, moved again and rubbed a tuft of hair between its thumb and toe. Satisfied, it laid hold of the bear skin, clenched its toes firmly round a curl or two and was still. Tuami was jerking like a man in a fit, the paddle was jerking and the parallel lines were spreading from the boat. The red leg was one of six that were creeping out of a crevice.

He cried out:

"What else could we have done?"

The mast and sail slid into focus. He saw that Marlan's eyes were open and could not tell how long they had been watching him.

Marlan spoke from deep inside his body.

"The devils do not like the water."

That was true, that was comfort. The water was miles wide and bright. Tuami looked imploringly at Marlan out of his pool. He forgot the dagger that was so nearly ground to a point.

"If we had not we should have died."

Marlan shifted restlessly, easing his bones from the hard wood. Then he looked at Tuami and nodded gravely.

The sail glowed red-brown. Tuami glanced back at the gap through the mountain and saw that it was full of golden light and the sun was sitting in it. As if they were obeying some signal the people began to stir, to sit up and look across the water at the green hills. Twal bent over Tanakil and kissed her and murmured to her. Tanakil's lips parted. Her voice was harsh and came from far away in the night.

"Liku!"

Tuami heard Marlan whisper to him from by the mast.

"That is the devil's name. Only she may speak it."

Now Vivani was really waking. They heard her huge, luxurious yawn and the bear skin was thrown off. She sat up, shook back her loose hair and looked first at Marlan then at Tuami. At once he was filled again with lust and hate. If she had been what she was, if Marlan, if her man, if she had saved her baby in the storm on the salt water——

"My breasts are paining me."

If she had not wanted the child as a plaything, if I had not saved the other as a joke——

He began to talk high and fast.

"There are plains beyond those hills, Marlan, for they grow less; and there will be herds for hunting. Let us steer in towards the shore. Have we water—but of course we have water! Did the women bring the food? Did you bring the food, Twal?"

Twal lifted her face towards him and it was twisted with grief and hate.

"What have I to do with food, master? You and he gave my child to the devils and they have given me back a changeling who does not see or speak."

The sand was swirling in Tuami's brain. He thought in panic: they have given me back a changed Tuami; what shall I do? Only Marlan is the same—smaller, weaker but the same. He peered forrard to find the changeless one as something he could hold on to. The sun was blazing on the red sail and Marlan was red. His arms and legs were contracted, his hair stood out and his beard, his teeth were wolf's teeth and his eyes like blind stones. The mouth was opening and shutting.

"They cannot follow us, I tell you. They cannot pass over water."

Slowly the red mist faded and became a sail glowing in the sun. Vakiti crawled round the mast, still carefully preserving the magnificent hair of which he was so proud from contact with the sheets which would have disarranged it. He slid round Marlan, conveying as much as the narrow boat would allow his respect for him and his regret for having to come so close. He picked his way past Vivani and came aft to Tuami, grinning ruefully.

"I am sorry, master. Now sleep."

He took the steering paddle under his left arm and settled down in Tuami's place. Released, Tuami crawled over Tanakil and knelt by the full pot, yearning at it. Vivani was doing her hair, arms up, comb drawing across, down, out. She had not changed, or at least only in respect of the little devil who owned her. Tuami remembered the night in Tanakil's eyes and put aside the thought of sleep. Presently perhaps, when he had to, but with the pot to help him. His restless hands felt at his belt and drew out the sharpening ivory with the shapeless haft. He found the stone in his pouch and began to grind, and there was silence. The wind freshened a little and the paddle made a rushing sound in their wake. The dug-out was so heavy that it would not lift or keep up with the wind as boats sometimes did if they were made of bark. So the wind blew round them warmly and took with it some of the confusion in his mind. He worked unhappily at the blade of his dagger and did not care whether he finished it or not but it was something to do.

Vivani finished with her hair and looked round at them all. She gave a little laugh that would have been nervous in anyone but Vivani. She pulled the cord that held the leathern cradle of her breasts and let the sun shine on them. Behind her Tuami could see the low hills and the green of trees with the darkness under them. The darkness stretched along above the water like a thin line and above it the trees were green and lively.

Vivani bent down and twitched aside the fold of bearskin. The little devil was there on a pelt, hands and feet holding tight. As the light poured over him he lifted his head off the fur and blinked his eyes open. He got up on his forelegs and looked round, brightly, solemnly, with quick movements of his neck and body. He yawned so that they could see how his teeth were coming and then a pink tongue whipped along his lips. He sniffed, turned, ran at Vivani's leg and scrambled up to her breast. She was shuddering and laughing as if this pleasure and love were also a fear and a torment. The devil's hands and feet had laid hold of her. Hesitating, half-ashamed, with that same frightened laughter, she bent her head, cradled him with her arms and shut her eyes. The people were grinning at her too as if they felt the strange, tugging mouth, as if in spite of them there was a well of feeling opened in love and fear. They made adoring and submissive sounds, reached out their hands, and at the same time they shuddered in replusion at the too-nimble feet and the red, curly hair. Tuami, his head full of swirling sand, tried to think of the time when the devil would be full grown. In this upland country, safe from pursuit by the tribe but shut off from men by the devil-haunted mountains, what sacrifice would they be forced to perform to a world of confusion? They were as different from the group of bold hunters and magicians who had sailed up the river towards the fall as a soaked feather is from a dry one. Restlessly he turned the ivory in his hands. What was the use of sharpening it against a man? Who would sharpen a point against the darkness of the world?

Marlan spoke hoarsely out of some meditation.

"They keep to the mountains or the darkness under the trees. We will keep to the water and the plains. We shall be safe from the tree-darkness."

Without being conscious of what he did, Tuami looked again at the line of darkness that curved away under the trees as the shore receded. The devil brat had had enough. He climbed down Vivani's wincing body and dropped into the dry bilges. He began to crawl inquisitively, propped on his forearms and peering about through eyes full of sunlight. The people shrank and adored, giggled and clenched their fists. Even Marlan shifted his feet and tucked them under him.

The morning was in full swing and the sun poured down at them from over the mountains. Tuami gave up his rubbing of stone against bone. He felt under his hand the shapeless lump that would be the haft of the knife when it was finished. There was no power in his hands and no picture in his head. Neither the blade nor the haft was important in these waters. For a moment he was tempted to throw the thing overboard.

Tanakil opened her mouth and made her mindless syllables.

"Liku!"

Twal flung herself howling across her daughter, holding the body close as if trying to reach the child who had left it.

The sand was back in Tuami's brain. He squatted, moving himself from side to side and turning the ivory aimlessly in his hand. The devil examined Vivani's foot.

There came a sound from the mountains, a tremendous noise that boomed along them and spread in a tangle of vibrations across the glittering water. Marlan was crouched, making stabbing motions at the mountains with his fingers, and his eyes were glaring like stones. Vakiti had ducked so that the paddle had swung them off the wind and the sail was rattling. The devil shared in all this confusion. He climbed rapidly up Vivani's body, through her hands that were spread instinctively to ward off, and then was burrowing into the hood of fur that lay behind her head He fell in and was confined. The hood struggled.

The noise from the mountains was dying away. The people, released as if a lifted weapon had been lowered, turned their relief and laughter on the devil. They shrieked at the struggling lump. Vivani's back was arched and she was writhing as though a spider had got inside her furs. Then the devil appeared, arse-upward, his little rump pushing against the nape of her neck. Even the sombre Marlan twisted his weary face into a grin. Vakiti could not straighten course for his wild laughing and Tuami let the ivory drop from his hands. The sun shone on the head and the rump and quite suddenly everything was all right again and the sands had sunk back to the bottom of the pool. The rump and the head fitted each other and made a shape you could feel with your hands. They were waiting in the rough ivory of the knife-haft that was so much more important than the blade. They were an answer, the frightened, angry love of the woman and the ridiculous, intimidating rump that was wagging at her head, they were a password. His hands felt for the ivory in the bilges and he could feel in his fingers how Vivani and her devil fitted it.

At last the devil was turned round and settled. He poked his head over her shoulder, keeping close, he nestled it against her neck. And the woman rubbed her cheek sideways against the curly hair, giggling and looking defiantly at the people. Marlan spoke in the silence.

"They live in the darkness under the trees."

Holding the ivory firmly in his hands, feeling the onset of sleep, Tuami looked at the line of darkness. It was far away and there was plenty of water in between. He peered forward past the sail to see what lay at the other end of the lake, but it was so long, and there was such a flashing from the water that he could not see if the line of darkness had an ending.

223

ff

Lord of the Flies

A plane crashes on a desert island and the only survivors, a group of schoolboys, assemble on the beach and wait to be rescued. By day they inhabit a land of bright fantastic birds and dark blue seas, but at night their dreams are haunted by the image of a terrifying beast. As the boys' delicate sense of order fades, so their childish dreams are transformed into something more primitive, and their behaviour starts to take on a murderous, savage significance.

The Inheritors

This was a different voice; not the voice of the people. It was the voice of other.

When the spring came the people moved back to their familiar home. But this year strange things were happening – inexplicable sounds and smells; unexpected acts of violence; and new, unimaginable creatures half-glimpsed through the leaves. Seen through the eyes of a small tribe of Neanderthals whose world is hanging in the balance, *The Inheritors* explores the emergence of a new race – ourselves, *Homo sapiens* – whose growing dominance threatens an entire way of life.

ff

Pincher Martin

Drowning in the freezing North Atlantic, Christopher Hadley Martin, temporary lieutenant, happens upon a grotesque rock, an island that appears only on weather charts. To drink there is a pool of rain water; to eat there are weeds and sea anemones. Through the long hours with only himself to talk to, Martin must try to assemble the truth of his fate, piece by terrible piece. *Pincher Martin* is a terrifying and unforgettable journey into one man's mind.

The Pyramid

Oliver is eighteen, and wants to enjoy himself before going to university. But this is the 1920s, and he lives in Stilbourne, a small English country town, where everyone knows what everyone else is getting up to, and where love, lust and rebellion are closely followed by revenge and embarrassment. Written with great perception and subtlety, *The Pyramid* is William Golding's funniest and most light-hearted novel, which probes the painful awkwardness of the late teens, the tragedy and farce of life in a small community and the consoling power of music.

ff

Free Fall

Somehow, somewhere, Sammy Mountjoy lost his freedom, the faculty of freewill 'that cannot be debated but only experienced, like a colour or the taste of potatoes'. As he retraces his life in an effort to discover why he no longer has the power to choose and decide for himself, the narrative moves between England and a prisoner-of-war camp in Germany. In *Free Fall*, his fourth novel, William Golding has created a poetic fiction, and an allegory, as moving as it is unforgettable.

The Spire

Dean Jocelin has a vision: that God has chosen him to erect a great spire on his cathedral. His mason anxiously advises against it, for the old cathedral was built without foundations. Nevertheless, the spire rises octagon upon octagon, pinnacle by pinnacle, until the stone pillars shriek and the ground beneath it swims. Its shadow falls ever darker on the world below, and on Dean Jocelin in particular.

ff

Darkness Visible

Darkness Visible opens at the height of the London Blitz, when a naked child steps out of an all-consuming fire. Miraculously saved but hideously scarred, soon tormented at school and at work, Matty becomes a wanderer, a seeker after some unknown redemption. Two more lost children await him, twins as exquisite as they are loveless. Toni dabbles in political violence, Sophy in sexual tyranny. As Golding weaves their destinies together, his book reveals both the inner and outer darkness of our world.

Rites of Passage

Sailing to Australia in the early years of the nineteenth century, Edmund Talbot keeps a journal to amuse his godfather back in England. Full of wit and disdain, he records the mounting tensions on the ancient, sinking warship where officers, sailors, soldiers and emigrants jostle in the cramped spaces below decks. Then a single passenger, the obsequious Reverend Colley, attracts the animosity of the sailors, and in the seclusion of the fo'castle something happens to bring him into a 'hell of degradation', where shame is a force deadlier than the sea itself.

ff

Close Quarters

In a wilderness of heat, stillness and sea mists, a ball is held on a ship becalmed halfway to Australia. In this surreal, fête-like atmosphere the passengers dance and flirt, while beneath them thickets of weed like green hair spread over the hull. The sequel to *Rites of Passage*, *Close Quarters*, the second volume in Golding's acclaimed *Sea Trilogy*, is imbued with his extraordinary sense of menace. Half-mad with fear, with drink, with love and opium, everyone on this leaky, unsound hulk is 'going to pieces'. And in a nightmarish climax the very planks seem to twist themselves alive as the ship begins to come apart at the seams.

Fire Down Below

The third volume of William Golding's acclaimed *Sea Trilogy*. A decrepit warship sails on the last stretch of its voyage to Sydney Cove. It has been blown off course and battered by wind, storm and ice. Nothing but rope holds the disintegrating hull together. And after a risky operation to reset its foremast with red-hot metal, an unseen fire begins to smoulder below decks.

ff

Faber and Faber – a home for writers

Faber and Faber is one of the great independent publishing houses in London. We were established in 1929 by Geoffrey Faber and our first editor was T. S. Eliot. We are proud to publish prize-winning fiction and non-fiction, as well as an unrivalled list of modern poets and playwrights. Among our list of writers we have five Booker Prize winners and eleven Nobel Laureates, and we continue to seek out the most exciting and innovative writers at work today.

www.faber.co.uk – a home for readers

The Faber website is a place where you will find all the latest news on our writers and events. You can listen to podcasts, preview new books, read specially commissioned articles and access reading guides, as well as entering competitions and enjoying a whole range of offers and exclusives. You can also browse the list of Faber Finds, an exciting new project where reader recommendations are helping to bring a wealth of lost classics back into print using the latest on-demand technology.